IRON EYES UNCHAINED

The notorious bounty hunter known as Iron Eyes is tracking down his errant sweetheart Squirrel Sally, and his quest takes him all the way from Mexico to the forests of the West. However, unbeknown to him, unscrupulous men envious of his success in his profession are pursuing him with a view to a kill. Iron Eyes is unwittingly riding into the jaws of Hell itself and will not survive unless divine intervention comes to his rescue. The problem is, only the Devil knows where he's gone . . .

RORY BLACK

---◆---

IRON EYES UNCHAINED

Complete and Unabridged

LINFORD
Leicester

First published in Great Britain in 2017 by
Robert Hale
an imprint of The Crowood Press
Wiltshire

First Linford Edition
published 2020
by arrangement with
The Crowood Press
Wiltshire

A catalogue record for this book is available
from the British Library.

ISBN 978–1–4448–4494–8

Published by
Ulverscroft Limited
Anstey, Leicestershire

Set by Words & Graphics Ltd.
Anstey, Leicestershire
Printed and bound in Great Britain by
T. J. International Ltd., Padstow, Cornwall

This book is printed on acid-free paper

1

The blistering heat of Mexico was far behind the emaciated horseman as he continued to follow the trail left by the feisty female he called Squirrel Sally. Young Sally Cooke had learned well from her mentor and knew every trick in the book of how to keep one step ahead of the gaunt horseman. Sally was teaching Iron Eyes a lesson. After months of tracking him, now he had to track her. She was only too aware that the infamous bounty hunter would not have even bothered to give chase if she had not pocketed his one hundred fresh-minted golden eagles before setting out on her battered stagecoach.

Iron Eyes had ignored her for far too long and she had to get his attention and teach him a lesson. As she cracked her bullwhip above the heads of her six-horse team she knew that nothing

1

focused the mind of the devilish bounty hunter like money.

His money.

The beautiful youngster had outwitted Iron Eyes and absconded with the precious hundred golden eagles he had earned by saving the life of Don Luis Fernandez's daughter over a month earlier. Notorious bounty hunter Iron Eyes had courageously laid his very life on the line and ridden into the secret stronghold of the Apache rebel Running Wolf in order to pluck the little girl from his clutches.

Yet upon returning to the hacienda of the Mexican nobleman with not only Fernandez's daughter but also a handful of other female captives in tow, Iron Eyes discovered that Sally had told Don Jose that she was his betrothed and taken the small fortune and fled upon her stagecoach.

Sally knew that stealing his hard-earned money was sure to get her the attention she craved from the man she was besotted with. Although most folks were terrified to even look at the mutilated features of Iron Eyes, Sally saw something else in his face. It was as though she had the ability to see beneath the brutal scars that covered his face and body. Sally was able to see the real Iron Eyes hidden deep in the depths of his tortured persona.

With the expertise that she had learned from the master hunter himself, Sally had evaded Iron Eyes far longer than even she had considered possible. Days had turned into weeks, which soon became over a month and yet the infamous man, known to many as the living ghost, was no closer to his goal.

Squirrel Sally had used the terrain to her advantage and guided her six-horse team on a path that even the bounty hunter found hard to track. Iron Eyes was riled by the perky young female's actions but in truth he was far angrier with himself than he could ever be with her.

Sally had done exactly as he would have done. She had beaten him to the punch and taken the money and ridden north just as he intended to do. The sly Sally had outwitted him yet again.

What angered Iron Eyes the most was that he had forsaken the large reward on the Apache rebel and left Running Wolf to rot where he had killed him.

The one hundred golden eagles that Don Jose had promised Iron Eyes seemed more than ample to compensate for losing the high bounty offered by the US Army. It would have been if his annoying female follower had not intercepted it. Yet like a hound on the trail of a racoon, he could not quit his hunting.

The skeletal rider had already crossed the Arizona territory and still had not caught even a glimpse of the golden-haired Sally or her unusual choice of vehicle. The arid landscape was far behind Iron Eyes and now he was entering a terrain that was unfamiliar to him. Snow-capped mountain peaks rose in the distance unlike anything Iron Eyes had ever seen before. Between the head of his sturdy palomino stallion and the rocky peaks, a sea of trees faced him.

Iron Eyes knew that he was still on her trail but for the life of him could not understand where Squirrel Sally was leading him. This was not a place where the gaunt hunter of men felt comfortable.

His narrowed eyes darted around him in search of the numerous dangers his guts were telling him might be behind every tree. His bony fingers teased his reins as the tall stallion trotted ever onward.

'I don't like this place, horse,' he muttered as his long skeletal fingers teased the pair of Navy Colts poking their grips from behind his belt buckle. 'It ain't healthy. Where the hell is Squirrel leading me?'

The massive palomino beneath the scarred figure had not put a foot wrong in the weeks since its master had set out from Fernandez's hacienda, yet even it was showing signs of weariness.

Iron Eyes knew that if he did not catch up with the impish female soon, he was going to have to stop and allow his powerful mount to recover from its unceasing labours. Unlike all of his previous mounts, the ruthless bounty hunter prized this animal. The golden stallion had a turn of foot that Iron Eyes knew had saved his bacon on more than one occasion. The last thing he wanted was for the palomino to drop dead beneath its ornate Mexican saddle.

Iron Eyes knew that horses like his golden stallion would keep running until their hearts burst. This was no place to be without a horse, he thought. The scarred face of the bounty hunter glanced around the trail through which he was riding.

A million trees flanked the twenty foot wide trail that his mount was trotting along. Iron Eyes pulled back on his long leathers and halted the lathered-up stallion. The thankful animal snorted long and hard as the bounty hunter glanced around the scene. When satisfied that there was no immediate danger, he threw his long leg over the horse's cream-coloured mane and slid to the ground.

The tall, lean figure rested his hands on his gun grips as his icy stare looked around the area. His honed instincts surveyed the area like a ravenous mountain lion seeking out its prey in readiness of striking yet there was nothing to alert the bounty hunter. No matter how hard he strained to locate the potential danger he was certain was out there, he could neither see nor hear anything. Finally he relaxed and glanced at the weary horse beside his bony shoulder.

'This place troubles me, horse,' he admitted.

The stallion nodded its head up and down as though in agreement. The almost white mane floated in the crisp air like the sails of a clipper.

Iron Eyes knelt and brushed the sandy ground with the palm of his bony hand and read every detail. The deep wheel grooves left by the stagecoach were still in pristine condition since Sally had driven her stagecoach this way. Iron Eyes rose back up to his full height and shook his head. He was utterly frustrated by the fact that the young female who he refused to admit caring for, was still winning this game of cat and mouse. He kicked at the dust.

'Damn it all,' he cursed. 'Squirrel is even tougher to catch than she is to shake off.'

Iron Eyes checked the canteens hanging from the ornate silver saddle horn until he located one still full of water and then removed it. He stood and unscrewed its stopper before removing the sombrero he had been wearing since leaving Mexico. He placed it at the stallion's feet and filled its bowl with the warm liquid.

'Drink up, horse,' he said as he returned the stopper to the canteen and then hung it back against the palomino's sturdy shoulders.

As the horse obeyed, Iron Eyes pulled a long slim cigar from his pocket and bit off its tip. He spat at the sand and then poked it between his teeth and searched for a match in his deep, bullet-filled pockets.

His thumbnail scratched the surface of the match. As it ignited into flame he cupped it in his hands and filled his lungs with smoke.

A million thoughts flashed through his mind as they had done since he had first set out after the stagecoach. So many thoughts of what he was going to do when he caught up with the elusive little Sally. They had grown with every passing day of his vain pursuit until he could no longer remember them all. All he knew for sure was that he intended to kick her rump, but was beginning to doubt that he would ever get the chance.

Had it not been for the one hundred golden eagles she had pocketed, he would not have given chase. At least that was what he told himself as smoke drifted from his mouth and hung in the morning air.

Iron Eyes watched the horse drink and then concentrated on the forest which surrounded him. As he inhaled on the cigar, he once again wondered why this place seemed different to any other he had ever travelled through.

He had grown to adulthood in a forest but it was nothing like this one, he mused. He scratched his cheek with his thumbnail and looked all around him. The trees looked nothing like those he had seen in other places. There was something strange about this place, he thought. An eerie trepidation gnawed at his craw as he stood beside the drinking horse and brooded. Smoke drifted from his mouth as he continued to glance over the shoulders of his high-shouldered mount.

'That silly little Squirrel is headed into something damn dangerous by my figuring, horse,' he said dryly and then glancing along the wide trail carved through the ocean of trees. 'We'd better find that

10

cantankerous gal before somebody else does.'

He shivered and then noticed that the stallion had finished drinking and raised its handsome head.

Iron Eyes scooped the sombrero up and shook it before returning it to his mane of long black hair. He lifted the stirrup and tightened the cinch strap before lowering the fender and reaching to the shinning saddle horn.

He lifted his left leg, poked the pointed toe of his mule-eared boot into the stirrup and pulled his lean frame off the ground. His long right leg cleared the cantle and then found the other stirrup.

'I don't like this place, horse,' he said in a low drawl as he gathered the reins in his bony hands. 'I sure hope Squirrel don't lead me into trouble. I've had my fill of trouble.'

Iron Eyes looked around the area for the umpteenth time and sighed heavily. He prepared to continue on his quest and leaned back against his saddle cantle.

'Git moving, horse,' he rasped.

Suddenly without warning the ear-splitting sound of a shot rang out and echoed all around the area. The bounty hunter flinched and stared in bewilderment at the tree tops as hundreds of surprised birds rose up into the morning sky and flew in all directions.

2

The muscular horse spooked. It required every ounce of Iron Eyes' strength to hold the startled palomino stallion in check as the unexpected sound slowly evaporated. Then another equally startling shot resonated and washed over the countless trees. The wide-eyed horse rose up and kicked out at the air as though battling some unseen force. Iron Eyes clung on to his massive mount as it stood on its hind legs and punched its hoofs at the morning air. The bounty hunter was almost unseated as the stallion came down heavily.

The narrowed eyes of the skeletal horseman darted around the trees for a mere hint of gun-smoke which might betray where the shooter was. Yet no matter how hard he squinted into the morning sunshine, he saw nothing.

Dust rose up from around the horse's

hoofs as Iron Eyes swung on his saddle, and looked behind them. The scarred horseman could not tell where the shooting was coming from. Another shot rang out but the before he could search for it, the skittish horse lifted off the ground and bucked. Its hind legs kicked out as it battled with its unseen attacker. Once again, Iron Eyes had to use every ounce of his dwindling strength to control the terrified animal as he fought with the bucking palomino. He grappled with his long leathers and eventually brought the snorting horse under control. Panting like an exhausted hound dog, the gaunt figure gritted his teeth and slapped the horse's ears.

'Will you quit trying to throw me, horse?' he shouted. 'I'm too tuckered for this kinda nonsense.'

The stallion settled and lowered its head as its master checked his lean frame for any hint of blood. He wondered if he might have been the target for somebody with his mind set on killing. His bony hands inspected every inch of his lean frame in search of a bullet hole and blood.

There was none.

'At least we ain't what that varmint's shooting at, horse,' he announced before drawing the reins close to his chest and slapping the stallion's ears again. 'Calm down. The last horse that bucked me like that got a bullet between his eyes. Don't go pushing your luck, pretty boy. I still got me plenty of ammunition and I'm loco enough to use it.'

The powerful horse shied as if it understood every word its horrific master uttered.

Holding the golden stallion in check, Iron Eyes looked up at the long winding trail road and then at the trees, which the countless black birds had abandoned as the reverberations of the gunshots faded into the distance. The lethal bounty hunter could not understand where the gunfire had come from or who its intended target was but he had a good idea. Sally was out there somewhere and that troubled Iron Eyes.

He knew only too well that she drew men's attention like flies to a dung heap. His little Squirrel was handsome in many men's eyes and that was a recipe for trouble in the West. She was also a crack-shot with her Winchester. Whoever had fired the three shots was unknown, but the dishevelled horseman had a good idea.

Sally was either fending off unwanted advances, killing game for her next meal or being used for target practice by those who wanted to get their hands on her six-horse team and stagecoach.

Any of the theories could be the correct one, but that did not diminish the gut feeling that there was something even more troublesome out there amid the trees. A potential danger he had not yet considered.

The bounty hunter sat astride the tall palomino and awaited the next shot to ring out in the quiet wilderness. It did not come. He kept turning the horse as his narrowed eyes searched for a sign of where the shot had originated. Once again he was not granted resolution.

Iron Eyes needed a target to aim for. He just needed a clue that would betray where the shots had come from. His eyes hungered for a mere glimpse of a wisp of gunsmoke hanging on the air, but there was none. Whoever had fired those shots was far from where he sat with his hand resting upon the grip of his closest Navy Colt.

He patted the neck of the tall stallion. His attention was drawn along the rough trail road that had been carved out of the forest. 'I got me a feeling in my craw that the shooting came from up there some place, horse. The same place that dumb-ass Squirrel is headed.'

Iron Eyes resolved that he would never see Sally or his one hundred golden eagles again unless he continued on into the depths of the unknown forested hills. He spat the chewed up remnant of the cigar at the ground and then wiped his mouth on the back of his sleeve.

His mind raced as it was tormented

by the thoughts that haunted him. Like so many others of his profession, the thought of losing the small fortune he had earned south of the border was too much to contemplate — yet it was something far more basic that had kept him following the fiery female. Something he would never admit to anyone, let alone himself.

Whatever he said, the truth was that he needed Sally far more than he needed the golden coins she had taken from him back in Mexico. Men of his profession could easily replace the money by killing another wanted outlaw and claiming the bounty upon their heads. It would have been impossible to replace Squirrel Sally and he knew it.

His bony hand reached back and pulled a whiskey bottle from his bags. His teeth gripped its cork and then extracted it before he spat it into the palm of his hand. He raised the bottle to his mutilated lips and drank as his thoughts dwelled upon the young female.

'That gal is like a rash,' he muttered as he allowed the whiskey to burn a trail down into his belly. 'She just keeps on itching at you. Squirrel don't let up.'

He returned the cork to the bottle neck and then slid the clear glass vessel back into his bags. He thought about how much money he had left and then checked the deep pockets of his trail coat. His spider-like fingers located a few silver coins amid the loose bullets.

His gruesome eyes stared at the coins, 'Damn it all. There's even less than I figured. I'd best catch up to that crazy minx damn fast. I ain't got enough money left to buy me a box of cigars let alone fill my bags with whiskey. This is getting serious.'

For the first time the skeletal bounty hunter was forced to admit that he was running low on money and provisions. His icy stare narrowed on the trail road. He had to find Squirrel Sally and retrieve the bag of golden coins.

There was no alternative. Not unless he intended going without cigars and gut-burning whiskey. He rubbed his jaw and thought about the shots he had just heard and pondered the fact that they seemed to be far closer than they actually were. His brutal eyes darted at the trees that flanked both sides of the crude trail road. Sound travelled unheeded along the valley between the high trees, he reasoned.

There was nothing to stop any noise from moving with the stiff breeze between the avenue of high firs and oaks. He straightened up on the palomino and started to nod as his razor-sharp spurs jabbed into the flanks of the stallion.

'Come on, horse,' he hissed as the powerful mount started to walk between the wheel rim grooves. 'We got us a real ornery little runt to catch.'

The horse started to trot.

'We gotta catch that gal mighty quick. We need the money she stole. I'm running out of whiskey and cigars, horse,' he snarled as he kept studying every shadow between the countless trees. 'If we don't rope Squirrel soon, we're as good as dead. I don't hanker to this place. It smells of death.'

His long hair flapped on his wide shoulders as the palomino gathered pace. Iron Eyes would have turned his large mount around and headed back to civilization had it not been for the hundred golden eagles Sally had taken.

Then another thought filled his weary mind.

What if it had been Squirrel Sally shooting at someone or something? She might be in trouble. She was a dead-shot just like him and usually hit what she was aiming at the first time. He had heard three shots being fired.

A bead of sweat trailed down his mutilated face.

'Squirrel don't waste lead,' he reminded himself. 'That could have bin her either shooting a critter for supper or putting an end to a varmint she took a dislike to.'

Iron Eyes jabbed his spurs into the flesh of the stallion. The high-shouldered horse started to canter as he raised his lean frame up and balanced in his stir-rups.

He rubbed beads of sweat from his upper lip and whipped the palomino's tail with his long leathers. The palomino started to gallop.

Within a mere heartbeat, the stallion was moving at pace along the wide trail road. As the horse quickened its speed, Iron Eyes glanced to both sides at the trees that flanked him.

The emaciated bounty hunter spat in anger and gripped the reins in his left hand whilst one of his Navy Colts filled the palm of the other. There still was no sign of anyone. A million thoughts raced through his mind as he glared from beneath the wide brim of the sombrero.

The stallion was now at full gallop.

Yet Iron Eyes demanded the powerful horse go faster. In the darkest recess of his weary soul he sensed that Squirrel Sally was in trouble.

His thin frame leaned over the neck of the racing stallion and continued to drive his spurs into the palomino's flanks.

The gaunt horseman knew that it was a race against time if his innards were right. The palomino stallion thundered along the trail road. It had never run as quickly before.

The bounty hunter was approaching a split in the trail road. It forked into two very different trails. One continued on up the tree covered mountain while the other disappeared down into a hollow. As he eased back on his reins and stared at the divided trail a series of shots rang out from the trees. This time they were closer.

Too close.

Iron Eyes felt the heat of the hot bullets as they passed within inches of him.

He dragged his long leathers to his left and spurred as he aimed the palomino at the lower road. The horse had only just managed to find its footing on the rough road when the bounty hunter felt his shoulder punched by one of the rifle bullets. He buckled but kept urging the stallion forward.

As the horse thundered down into the dense tree-lined hollow Iron Eyes glanced at his shoulder. The coat was ripped at the shoulder and droplets of blood were staining its fabric.

Iron Eyes slumped over the neck of his powerful horse and kept spurring. The bullets of unknown bushwhackers kept pace with his mount's every stride. Dust was kicked up into the air all around the hoofs of the stallion as the unknown riflemen tried to finish off the legendary bounty hunter.

3

Danger was growing ever closer to the skeletal horseman as he whipped his charging palomino in a bid to escape the bushwhacker's deadly bullets. Yet even wounded, Iron Eyes knew that no horse could ever outrun hot lead for long. Eventually his hidden foes would get him in their sights again and finish the job they had started.

Most men would have waited for that fateful bullet to end their misery, but Iron Eyes was not most men. For years he had ridden with impending death on his shoulder. It held no fear for the man considered already dead.

As the palomino stallion valiantly attempted to obey its master's vicious spurs, Iron Eyes was totally unaware who his attackers were even though they shared the same dubious profession.

Nothing could have warned Iron Eyes

that two men he had briefly encountered a week earlier in one of the many remote settlements dotted along the uncharted borders between the territories, had been lying in wait for him. The infamous bounty hunter, known to honest and dishonest men alike as Iron Eyes, would never have believed that men of his own bloody trade would knowingly attempt to slaughter him. Yet that was what they were trying to do.

Chet Simmons and his fellow bounty hunter Moses Carter had been drinking at the Silver Dollar Saloon when they spotted Iron Eyes as he purchased two bottles of rye whiskey before heading to the local hotel.

Although they had never met, there was no mistaking the ravaged figure of Iron Eyes. His description was vivid and both bounty hunters knew that no two men could look like he did. Although they had been across the saloon from Iron Eyes when he had purchased his daily ration of whiskey, Carter and Simmons suddenly realized who they were looking at.

Both men were correct in identifying the infamous bounty hunter but wrong about why he was in town. Neither realized that Iron Eyes was only trailing Squirrel Sally and not after the same outlaw bounties that they were hoping to get.

Simmons and Carter considered themselves his equal when in truth they were just pathetic copies. They were like so many others who plied their trade under the guise of acting for the general good. They killed because they enjoyed killing and savoured the rewards being bounty hunters brought them. The trouble was they considered Iron Eyes far too good a rival to tolerate.

It had been obvious to both the bounty hunters who the stranger was as soon as they had set eyes upon his horrific features. Only one man could look the way that Iron Eyes looked. They had heard that Iron Eyes face resembled a skull with skin stretched across its bony countenance. In reality it looked far worse.

Carter and Simmons had travelled fifty miles before arriving at Broken Spur in pursuit of the three wanted outlaws they intended claiming the bounty for.

To men like Simmons and Carter, seeing the notorious Iron Eyes was like a red rag to a bull. They had wrongly assumed that he was after the same outlaws as they were. Each knew that he was far more likely to catch the outlaws than they were.

That was something they could not allow to happen.

The numerous stories they had heard over the years of how others in their lethal trade had lost out to Iron Eyes' superior hunting skills gnawed at their craws.

They had spent far too much money trailing the trio of wanted outlaws to see the reward money go to the gaunt Iron Eyes.

As the skeletal figure had left the saloon Moses Carter and Chet Simmons brooded and planned over a further bottle of amber liquor as to how they could prevent the famed Iron Eyes from once again beating his fellow bounty hunters to the hefty reward money.

There was only one certain way to prevent Iron Eyes and that was to kill him. Neither of the bounty hunters shied away from executing anybody and Iron Eyes was no exception.

Just seeing him in Broken Spur had alerted the pair to the fact that if he continued on up into the mountainous forest after the Denver gang, they would lose the $5,000 bounty for sure.

'We gotta stop that bastard,' Simmons had snarled.

Carter had nodded in agreement. 'Yep, we gotta kill that critter before he catches up with Jody Denver and his boys and nabs them. Iron Eyes will steal that bounty from under our noses if we don't stop him.'

The pair was in total agreement as they left the saloon and wandered across the street toward the high-sided livery stable. The two ruthless gunmen checked with the blacksmith that Iron Eyes had left his prized stallion for the night.

Simmons had realized that they could get well ahead of the emaciated Iron Eyes if they set out for the tree-covered hills while he slept in his hotel room. Once there, they could lie in wait and kill the unsuspecting Iron Eyes when he appeared the following morning. They intended cutting him down in a lethal crossfire and stomping what was left into the ground until he was virtually unrecognizable. After that they could set out after the valuable outlaws unhampered.

It had been a simple plan.

If Iron Eyes were not in their equation it might have worked like all the other times they had ambushed their unsuspecting prey. The trouble was that Iron Eyes did not die easy. His painfully lean frame had a knack of escaping the majority of bullets that were fired at it.

Both men paid the blacksmith what they owed and led their mounts out into the quiet street. With Broken Spur bathed in darkness, they had hauled their drunken frames on to their horses and started to head along the main street toward the forest.

Fuelled by whiskey fumes, they knew that if they did not stop Iron Eyes, he would hunt down their prey before they even realized it. They had spent far too much money and time in their hunt for the Denver boys to see it squandered.

This was one bounty they had determined would not end up in Iron Eyes' pockets.

There was only one route up into the vast forest. A wide road carved out by loggers years earlier. Simmons and Carter agreed that Iron Eyes would have to take it.

As their mounts snorted beneath them, Carter and Simmons spurred and rode out of the remote settlement, they glanced at the hotel as they passed its wooden structure. One dimly lit lamp glowed behind the lace drape on the second floor.

'Reckon he's sleeping, Moses?' Simmons grunted as they had headed toward the trees that dominated the territory.

'I reckon so,' Carter nodded. 'It'll be the last damn sleep he gets before we cut him down to size.'

The bounty hunters spurred.

4

The powerful palomino had continued thundering along the sun baked trail road for more than ten minutes when it suddenly felt the weight fall from its high shoulders. Iron Eyes hit the ground hard as the whirlpool of sickening unconsciousness overwhelmed him. Yet unlike most normal men, the shock of hitting the solid ground woke him up. His eyes opened as he bounced over and over before finding his lean frame crashing into the brush.

Thorny bushes and tree trunks halted his progress after he hit the undergrowth. For a moment the bounty hunter just lay on his back and stared up at the dark branches that loomed over him. He blinked hard and then placed his bony hands on the treacherous ground. Thorns cut into the palms of his outstretched hands as he forced his emaciated body off the ground until he was in a sitting position.

As he stared through blurred eyes he could hear the sound of horses' hoofs pounding as they approached. Iron Eyes grabbed at a vine and hauled his bruised body upright and then fell against a damp tree trunk.

His dazed mind seemed incapable of clearing. Every bone in his body hurt as his stick-like digits pressed into his throbbing temples. An entire tribe of hostile Apaches were hammering war drums inside his pounding skull. He swung around on his boot leather and rested his back against the tree as he tried to gather his wits together.

'Wake up,' he mumbled to himself. 'This ain't over. You gotta fight them bastards if'n you intend catching up with little Squirrel.'

He opened his eyes again and stared through the blurred swirls of dancing colours in a bid to regain his sight. The sound of the horses' hoofs was getting louder.

Iron Eyes buried his face into his hands and rubbed his eye's hard. He opened them and blinked several times. The waterfall cleared and he was able to focus. The palomino stallion was standing thirty feet from him. The tall animal was staring back at him.

The emaciated bounty hunter went to walk toward it when he glanced over his right shoulder. Iron Eyes stopped in his tracks as he saw the two riders.

'Who the hell are they?' he muttered as he placed a hand on the tree and steadied himself.

Suddenly both horsemen opened fire with their repeating rifles. The ground was kicked up as Carter and Simmons tried to find their target again. Plumes of dust filled the air as the scent of acrid gunsmoke filled his flared nostrils.

Iron Eyes ducked as bullets hit the trunk and sent bark cascading over him. He dropped on to one knee as the mounted Simmons and Carter continued to fire their rifles at him.

The startled bounty hunter pulled

both his Navy Colts from his waist band and cocked their hammers in turn. He winced as riveting pain cut through his lean frame like a lightning strike. He had forgotten about the savage wound in his shoulder until this very moment.

He bent over and sucked in air.

Bullets tore up the ground all around him. Iron Eyes stared at the droplets of blood as they constantly dripped from his shoulder on to the sun-bleached ground. He gritted his teeth and then opened one eye and glared at the pair of riders.

'I ain't dead just yet,' he snarled defiantly. 'But you are.'

Then faster than spit he raised both hands and squeezed the triggers of his guns. Two rods of lethal lead spewed from the barrels of his weapons in deafening unison and carved through the sunshine.

He heard the sickening noise of one of the horses as both bullets caught the animal in its chest. Moses Carter felt the stricken horse buckle beneath him just before he flew over its head and crashed into the ground. Simmons hauled rein beside his companion and threw himself from his saddle. As Carter fought to get back off the ground, Simmons cranked the lever of his Winchester and levelled it at the infamous bounty hunter.

Simmons fired.

The fiery flame emerged from the Winchester barrel and hit the tail of Iron Eyes' trailing blood-stained dust coat. The bounty hunter blasted another shot at the men and then staggered backwards. Simmons unleashed a torrent of bullets at Iron Eyes as the bounty hunter miraculously tripped back to the trees. No swarm of crazed hornets could have sounded more fevered as the bullets cut through the dry mountain air.

The tall, scarred bounty hunter only just managed to get behind the sturdy trunk of a tree when the deadly bullets peppered its trunk.

Chunks of bark and burning sawdust exploded all around the weary figure as his thumbs dragged back on his gun hammers again. As the rifle fire momentarily stopped as Simmons was forced to reload, Iron Eyes fired blindly back along the trail road.

Yet neither side could see the other through the dense choking cloud of gunsmoke. Iron Eyes panted like a world-weary hound as his fingers pulled the spent bullet casings from the smoking chambers of one of his guns.

'I'm starting to get mighty angry with them bastards,' he whispered as he pushed his hand into his pocket and pulled out fresh ammunition.

Crouched behind the body of the dead horse Simmons reloaded his rifle with fresh bullets from his gun belt and pushed them into the rifle's magazine. Carter rubbed the blood from his face and crawled to his side. The stunned bounty hunter had smashed his nose into the unforgiving ground when he was thrown over the head of his stricken horse. Somehow he still had hold of his rifle as he crouched beside Simmons.

'What happened?' he asked as teeth fell from his bleeding mouth on to his shirt.

'Quit moaning and get shooting, Moses,' Simmons riled as his fingers searched for more bullets in his belt loops. 'We gotta kill that critter before he adds us to his tally of notches.'

'Reckon you're right, Chet,' Carter looked at his partner and cranked his rifle's mechanism. The injured bounty hunter started firing in Iron Eyes' direction. 'That varmint done killed my horse.'

Iron Eyes heard the remark above the sound of the Winchester's repeated blasts and chuckled to himself as he rested his bony spine against the tree trunk.

'Soon I'm gonna kill you too,' he hissed.

Simmons jerked the hand guard and sent a spent casing flying over his shoulder as he raised his rifle to his shoulder and looked along the gun sights.

'Don't go fretting none, you can have my nag once we've sent Iron Eyes to Hell, Moses,' Simmons drawled and fired his Winchester.

With blood dripping from his busted nose Carter lowered his rifle and looked at his partner. 'You're giving me your horse? How come?'

'I'm gonna be riding that tall golden horse yonder, Moses,' Simmons said confidently. 'Once we kill Iron Eyes, that is.'

Iron Eyes suddenly emerged from his place of cover and fanned his hammer. Two shots raced through the air and narrowly missed the bounty hunters sending them reeling backwards. With chunks of leather and sawdust covering them, they clambered behind the body of the dead horse and peeked over the saddle. Iron Eyes was gone again. Simmons clenched a fist and thumped the saddle. He then fired over the belly of the stricken horse to where gunsmoke still hung in the air.

There was no reply.

Simmons and Carter looked at one another. Neither could conceal their confusion. Both men remained trapped next to the dead horse for another five minutes. In all that time there were no replies to their shots. Finally Carter pulled blood clots from his broken nose and rubbed it on his pants leg.

'The bastard is playing with us, Chet,' he announced.

'Maybe he's running low on ammunition,' Simmons ventured as he cranked the Winchester's mechanism again. 'He might even be dead. I know that I hit him back there. I seen his scrawny hide buckle.'

Carter knelt in the horse's blood and peered over the saddle to where the shots had been coming from. He glanced at his partner and chewed on his gloved knuckle.

'He might be dead just like you reckoned, Chet,' he shrugged. 'It's hard to tell with Iron Eyes though. He looked dead when he was buying that whiskey back at Broken Spur.'

Simmons grinned and gripped his rifle. 'If he ain't dead now he sure will be, partner.'

'What you gonna do, Chet?'

Simmons started to nod to himself as he pulled out his pocket watch and studied its dial. 'In another five minutes I'm gonna rush him with my rifle spitting lead, Moses. I intend killing that varmint right now.'

Carter shrugged and again wiped his nose. It was starting to dawn on the bloody bounty hunter that trying to kill the infamous Iron Eyes was not such a good idea after all.

5

The distant sound of the shots echoed around the stagecoach as it travelled the perilous mountain road between the avenue of endless trees. Squirrel Sally pulled back on the hefty reins, then pressed her bare foot down on the brake pole and looked all around her. Yet there was no hint of where the shots had come from apart from the fact that they appeared to have emanated far behind the battered vehicle. The six horses started to slow as the feisty female knelt on the driver's board, looked over the roof and squinted through the brilliant sunshine in a vain attempt at finding answers to the burning questions which gnawed at her craw.

'Now who in tarnation is having themselves a war all the way out here?' she muttered to herself as the stagecoach continued to gradually slow. 'Them shots

I heard earlier was a whole heap closer. If I didn't know better I'd swear that I've driven this buggy into a hillbilly war.'

The normally calm youngster shivered as doubts started to creep into her mind. For the first time since she had set out from Mexico, Sally doubted the wisdom of her journey.

'Maybe it wasn't smart for me to tease old Iron Eyes like I done,' she sighed quietly as her beautiful eyes searched the surrounding terrain for possible danger. 'I got me a feeling that I ought to have stayed back at that fancy hacienda.'

The trail road, which had been wide enough for two wagons to pass one another a mile earlier, was now narrowing. She looked around her stationary stagecoach and toyed with the long leathers nervously before looping them around the brake pole.

The tree canopies were interlocked above her head and bathed the area in an eerie light better suited to night time rather than the middle of morning.

'For all I know Iron Eyes ain't within a hundred miles of here,' she told herself as she reached down into the driver's box, picked up a whiskey bottle and removed its cork. She took a swing, shuddered and then returned the cork to the neck of the bottle. The hard liquor did not make her feel any braver but, true to her nature, she refused to admit to herself that she was frightened.

But she was scared. Really scared.

Sally wiped her mouth on her tattered sleeve and then vainly attempted to pull the weathered shirt over her heaving bosom. She tutted and shook her head. No amount of adjustment seemed to work. Flesh that she managed to conceal simply enabled another part of her shapely form to escape.

'My chests are getting bigger,' she muttered to herself and then thought about Iron Eyes and smiled. 'I figure it's coz I'm betrothed. I ain't never seen a flat-chested married woman.'

Then she heard more shots as they echoed across the tops of the countless trees that were too close. With her trusty Winchester in her petite hands, she got to her feet and carefully walked across the top of the stagecoach. The sound of the gunfire was still ringing in her ears as she reached the rear of the vehicle.

Sally cranked the rifle guard and cocked the weapon. Her heart was pounding hard and fast inside her chest. She placed her left foot on the metal luggage rail that trimmed the stagecoach rooftop. The cold steel felt good against her skin as she studied the trail behind the long vehicle.

'Damn it all,' she cursed. 'How come there ain't nothing to be seen but a whole lot to be heard?'

The steel rims of the stagecoach's wheels skidded across the rough road as the snorting horses nervously moved between the traces. Sally steadied herself and then turned around and walked back to the seat. She stepped down and then sat again as the nervous team kept fighting their restraints.

'Quit that, you dumb gluepots,' she growled before resting the rifle across her lap and unlooping the reins from the brake pole. 'My ass is sore enough sitting on this damn plank without you making it worse.'

The ears of the horses sensed that the tiny female was not her usual perky self. Their ears pricked up as she began to pull back on the lengths of leathers in her hands and serenade them with whistles. Expertly, Sally managed to get the stagecoach to reverse until the trail was wide enough for her to attempt to turn it.

After more than ten minutes the stage-coach was facing in the opposite direction. Sally rested both her feet on the lip of the driver's board and exhaled deeply. The action had exhausted her but she knew that there was no point in trying to keep going along this ever-narrowing trail road. A solitary rider might be able to navigate a route through the forest but not the stagecoach.

Although Sally was unaware of the

fact that the road had originally been carved out by loggers to make it easier for them to load their wagons with freshly felled trees, she knew that whoever had created this road had abandoned it long ago. The forest had reclaimed the higher part of the trail and in time would also envelop the rest of it.

Sally realized that she had to return down the steep hillside and hope that she did not encounter the men who were firing their weaponry. Her blue eyes glanced to her right at the severe drop that started about three feet from the rough road.

Her tongue licked her dry lips.

'That's a mighty big drop,' she gulped. 'Reckon I'd best try and keep this crate on the road otherwise I'm gonna be playing a harp.'

The team were even less happy than she was. They had disturbed sharp thorns of bramble bushes and vines as Sally had carefully managed to turn the stagecoach around. The thorny vines cut into their flesh.

'Easy, boys,' Sally spat before placing her pipe between her lips and then striking a match and placing it over the corncob bowl. She puffed until smoke billowed from her mouth and then blew at the match's flame. The journey down the mountainside was going to take a long time and she knew it. It was one she did not care to start but as with all inevitable things she knew it was unavoidable. 'This is all Iron Eyes' fault. I wouldn't even be here if that scrawny galoot had paid me some attention back at the hacienda. Damn it all, don't he know that we is almost married?'

She glanced down at the leather sack in the driver's box and gave a satisfied chuckle. The rough leather bag gave no clue as to its contents, but she knew what she had. She had the one hundred golden eagles that belonged to Iron Eyes. For a moment she forgot about the fact that her flight had been violently stopped and she was being forced to retrace her tracks. Sally slapped her thigh and laughed out loud.

'That scrawny old scarecrow is gonna be mighty angry knowing I got his money,' she laughed and picked up the bag. She shook it against her ear. The sound of the golden coins trapped within the leather bag filled her with glee. 'Serves him right. It don't pay to ignore your betrothed. I figure this has taught him a lesson he ain't gonna forget in a hurry.'

Like a seasoned stagecoach driver, Sally released the brake and started to tease the hefty reins. Slowly but surely the horses started to walk. The sound of their chains rang out in the gloom as the long vehicle began the descent.

Wisps of dust drifted from the wheel rims as they skimmed the edge of the mountain trail and drifted in the thin air over the trees. Squirrel Sally was well aware that one mistake could send her and her stagecoach crashing off the mountain road and into the tree-covered abyss.

'Keep going, boys,' Sally told the

team as she tapped the long leathers on to the horses' backs, 'Nice and easy.'

Few grown men could have handled the six horses so skilfully yet with every step they took, Sally felt her heart quicken its pace. It took all her strength to keep the horses from charging downhill but she knew that was a recipe for disaster. She had to maintain a steady speed along the road as the stagecoach's wheels went within inches of the very edge of the deadly drop.

As the long vehicle slowly negotiated the perilous pathway downward, Sally continued to puff feverishly on her pipe and stare like a ravenous hawk through her loose golden curls at the horses. The last thing she wanted was for one of the team to veer too far to the very rim of the road. One false step could bring disaster and cause the entire six horses to fall to their deaths and take her and the coach with them.

'Keep moving, boys,' she urged in a voice intended to calm the powerful horses, 'That's it, nice and easy.'

6

Acrid grey gunsmoke drifted from the rifle barrels of the bounty hunters as they waited for the gaunt Iron Eyes to show himself and return fire, yet after more than five minutes had passed without any sign of their wounded prey Simmons and Carter began to get nervous. Carter crawled through the blood-covered ground to where Simmons knelt beside the saddle of the upturned horse.

'Where is he, Chet?' Carter frantically asked his partner as he placed his rifle barrel on the neck of the stricken horse. 'Where in tarnation has that Iron Eyes gone?'

'I figure he's behind that undergrowth riddled with bullet holes, Moses,' Simmons said as his fingers pulled the last of the bullets in his belt and slid them into the rifle's magazine.

'You still gonna charge him?'

'I'm thinking about it.'

Carter was soaked in his own gore as he rested his shoulder against the saddle. 'This was a mistake. We should have let Iron Eyes be. I'm telling you, Chet. We should ride out and leave him.'

Without taking his eyes off the dense undergrowth, Simmons hissed a reply and curled his finger around his rifle trigger. 'I reckon he's still there, Moses. He's wounded and probably hurt too bad to move. We've fired enough bullets into that brush to kill a grizzly bear. I reckon we've done for the varmint.'

Carter blasted another volley of lead into the place where they had last seen the infamous bounty hunter and then began pulling the last of his bullets from his belt and ramming them into the Winchester. He shook his head and moved closer to his companion.

'This is Iron Eyes we're hunting, Chet,' he drawled. 'He ain't no normal critter. Even wounded he's still the most danger-ous varmint we've ever tackled.'

Simmons kept staring at the sun-baked

trees. 'He's just a man like we are, Moses. He ain't nothing more. We wounded him and he's either suffering or winging it to Hell.'

Carter looked at the rest of the trees around them and started to shake his head again. He was scared and unable to hide the fact.

'I reckon he's moving around behind them trees waiting to get us in his gun sights,' he blurted out as his eyes darted at each of them in turn. 'I've heard about him. Iron Eyes ain't no normal man like us. They say he can't be killed 'coz he's already dead.'

'That's foolish talk, Moses,' Simmons shook his head as he concentrated on the place he had last caught sight of the emaciated bounty hunter. 'All men can die. Iron Eyes ain't no different to the rest of us. He's just a whole lot uglier than most, that's all. Quit fretting.'

Carter wanted to believe his fellow back-shooter but every second that passed seemed to make his fears grow. He looked at the high-shouldered palomino stallion that had not moved an inch from where they had first seen it. He rubbed the sweat from his whiskered mouth and exhaled.

Simmons looked at his partner, 'What's eating at you, Moses? You look plumb weird.'

Carter nodded in agreement as he pointed the barrel of his Winchester at the palomino standing twenty feet from where they had last seen Iron Eyes.

'That big golden horse ain't feared of shooting, Chet,' he noted. 'With all the gun play you'd think it would have run off for cover, but it just stands there.'

Simmons looked at the horse. 'Yeah, that is kinda strange. Most nags would have high-tailed as soon as the shooting started, but that big fella ain't even troubled by all the noise. I'm gonna enjoy owning that big fella.'

Suddenly the blood of both bounty hunters froze as they heard the haunting sound of spurs jangling behind them. They glanced at each other as a long dark shadow crept up between them and covered the dead horse they were huddled behind.

Then the shadow stopped moving and the spurs ceased ringing its deathly tune. Both Simmons and Carter tried to swallow, but fear had tightened its invisible noose around their throats. Their gloved hands gripped their rifles as they heard the distinctive sound of gun hammers being locked into position behind their backbones.

Simmons mouthed at Carter. 'Turn when I turn and start blasting.'

Moses Carter gave a single nod of his head.

Faster than the blink of an eye, they swung on their knees and faced the tall figure with their rifles levelled. Yet they paused as the reality of the horrific apparition filled them with total dread. Iron Eyes stood like something that had just crawled from their worst nightmares and towered over them. His mutilated face bore evidence of every battle he had fought and no longer resembled anything they had ever set eyes upon before.

Flesh had been stitched together crudely or allowed to mend unaided. Whatever Iron Eyes had once looked like was now a distant memory. His long limp black hair hung on his wide shoulders cradling the devilish image that the two men were staring up at in terror.

Although they had heard the descriptive stories about the mysterious ghostlike bounty hunter, neither could believe what they were looking at.

Nothing on the face of the earth should have looked the way that Iron Eyes looked. Nothing alive should have even come close to the way the emaciated bounty hunter appeared. Iron Eyes lowered his head and stared into his adversaries' eyes and recognized the shocked expressions etched upon them. He had seen it many times before.

'You had your chance,' he growled in his deep raspy voice.

Yellowish flames exploded from both barrels of his Navy Colts. The rods of death cut through the dry air and hit both kneeling men in their chests.

There was no emotion in their dispatch. Iron Eyes calmly stared at the gore-splattered bounty hunters and spat at them. Both men rocked on their knees as their rifles slipped from their hands a fraction of a heartbeat before they fell on to their faces at his boots.

'You should have fired,' Iron Eyes poked his smoking gun barrels into his waist band behind his belt buckle and then lifted their heads in turn to study their features. Whoever these men were, he did not recognize them. They did not resemble any of the wanted poster images on the crumpled posters in his pockets. 'Damn it all. Whoever these hombres were they ain't got bounty on them. I hate wasting lead on worthless back-shooters. There ain't no profit in it.'

Iron Eyes straightened up to his full height and removed the wide-brimmed sombrero from his head to reveal his tortured features. The sun felt good as it burned into his face whilst his eyes darted to his painful shoulder. The padding of his dust coat was hanging from where the bullet had torn through it and grazed him. He glanced down at his hand poking from the sleeve of his coat and flexed his long fingers. Blood still dripped from his claw-like digits.

The sight of his own blood riled Iron Eyes. He furiously grabbed both bodies and viciously turned them over on to their backs. Within seconds he had riffled every pocket in search of any money they were carrying.

As his long skinny legs strode back to where his horse awaited its master, Iron Eyes counted the money. Two hundred and fifty-three dollars was the tally.

'At least it wasn't a total loss,' he grunted before folding the bills and pushing them into his vest pocket. As his mind wondered who they were, he snatched the long leathers hanging from the palomino's bridle and grabbed the stallion's mane. 'I reckon they were just two dumb road agents figuring on stealing every penny they could get their hands on from anyone passing along this trail road.'

Iron Eyes hung the sombrero from his saddle-horn and then raised his leg and poked the boot into the stirrup. He stared through the sickening heat haze at the dead men and shook his head.

'Reckon you boys didn't know that Squirrel Sally had already robbed me,' he snarled and touched his brow in mocking salute. 'Thank you kindly for the donation, brothers. I'll be thinking about you the next time I buy me some whiskey.'

He mounted and collected his reins in his hands and abruptly turned the horse. As he pondered the trail that snaked up through the overwhelming trees, his thoughts returned to the hapless bounty hunters.

'What the hell were they doing all the way out here?' he sighed and poked a cigar between his teeth. He then scratched a match across the silver horn of his saddle and raised it to the tip of the twisted weed between his teeth. 'And why were they shooting at me? If I was gonna ambush anyone I'd do it closer to a saloon. This country ain't fit for man or beast.'

Smoke filled his lungs as he tossed the dead match at the equally dead bounty hunters. The pain in his shoulder still burned like a wildfire but he did not have time to waste tending his wound. He still had to find Squirrel Sally and get his golden eagles out of her feminine clutches.

Iron Eyes was about to spur when more distant shots rang out from up in the depths of the forest. He raised his deathly head and stared through the strands of his long limp hair. His eyes narrowed as he focused. He frowned.

'Looks like we still ain't on our lonesome, horse,' he hissed and slapped the tail of his reins across the palomino's shoulders. The powerful stallion responded and started to trot along the trail. As the palomino began to find more speed, Iron Eyes replaced the spent bullets from his guns with fresh ones from his deep coat pockets in readiness for the next varmints to try their luck and stop his progress. With the mangled cigar gripped between his teeth, Iron Eyes was well aware that whoever had fired the shots he had heard were probably far more dangerous than the bodies behind him.

They were still alive.

'Not for long.' He smirked to himself. 'Not for long.'

7

Like something that had just crawled from the fiery bowels of Hell, the battle-scarred bounty hunter continued to drive the muscular mount ever onward. There was fire in his eyes as well as his belly. Something was driving him on after the tiny stagecoach driver and it had nothing to do with the small fortune in golden coins that she had intercepted before Iron Eyes had returned to Don Jose Fernandez's magnificent hacienda.

Although the gaunt horseman did not recognize the feelings that fuelled his quest, Iron Eyes was certain that he had to catch up with Squirrel Sally before something bad happened to her. At first he had attempted to dismiss the fateful thoughts that hung over him like an executioner's axe, yet no matter how hard he tried, Iron Eyes could not shake off the dread which haunted him.

Although Squirrel Sally did not realise it, she was a very good-looking young female who had a knack of attracting the wrong sort of attention. Iron Eyes felt that she was vulnerable to the depraved desires of most who set eyes upon her. This mixed with the fact that she was alone in a perilous land that harboured many unseen dangers from not only the varied wildlife but also the two-legged type.

As he spurred his powerful stallion on, Iron Eyes had completely forgotten why he had originally started out after her. Now he was driven by the uncontrollable thoughts which he was unable to shake off.

All the bounty hunter knew for sure was that he had to catch up with the stubborn Squirrel before fate dealt her a lethal hand of aces and eights — the death hand made famous by being the fateful cards Wild Bill Hickok had been holding when killed in Deadwood.

The Grim Reaper had many guises

and Iron Eyes knew that every one of them was deadly. His feelings for Squirrel Sally out-weighed any consideration for his own safety. Every fibre of his being told him that he had to locate the female he normally tried to flee.

He whipped and spurred his mount along the lower trail relentlessly as blood continued to stream down from the deep graze on his shoulder. Yet Iron Eyes ignored the savage injury and the pain that would have felled a lesser man. The infamous bounty hunter had only one thought in his mind and that was to catch up with the besotted Squirrel Sally before she became just another notch on the Grim Reaper's long list of casualties.

The golden horse obeyed every demand its master made of it and ploughed down through a dense gully of flesh-ripping brambles until its hoofs located solid ground again.

Yet if Iron Eyes had been his usual self, he might have realized that he was far from alone in the forested trail. The two men he had killed were now far behind him lying beneath a sun nearly as merciless as himself, but there were other men in the forest. Men who, like himself, feared nothing. Men who had good reason to hate and kill those who invaded their last refuge.

Iron Eyes rode along the ever-narrowing trail and stared unblinking at what lay ahead. As his blood-stained spurs continued to urge the exhausted stallion on, he was totally unaware that a dozen sets of eyes were following his every movement. Just as they had done since he had first entered the uncharted forest.

Yet his observers were not what he had even imagined existed in this remote part of the territory. Had Iron Eyes been more aware of what surrounded him, he might have spotted them as they silently kept pace with him.

Sat astride their small colourful ponies, the small hunting party of Kiowa warriors had watched his every move from the cover of the countless trees and virtually impenetrable undergrowth. Their sharp eyesight had witnessed many men enter the forest over the years, but the sight of Iron Eyes was different.

He was the living nightmare they had heard about from their elders. A creature which barely resembled a real man any longer and had become almost mythical in the telling and retelling of his encounters with other tribes.

Unknown to Iron Eyes, the twelve highly-painted horsemen had been out hunting fresh game to take back to their encampment deep in the uncharted wilderness when they had first become aware of the bounty hunter riding along the trail road. The warriors had been tracking deer to feed their young and old when they had spotted the grotesque Iron Eyes.

They had used the cover of the dense forest to secretly keep pace with the haunting figure as he spurred on toward the fork in the trail where the Kiowa had already spotted Simmons and Carter lying in wait.

The bushwhacking crossfire had not worked.

As the gunsmoke cleared, the collection of braves had watched as Simmons and Carter had chased the wounded creature along the lower trail road with rifles blazing. The warriors had remained hidden from view as the bounty hunters bore down on their hideous prey.

Their suspicions of who was the rider of the magnificent palomino stallion were confirmed when, after being cut down by the back-shooter's repeating rifles, Iron Eyes somehow rose like a phoenix and dished out his own brand of merciless retribution.

Only one creature was capable of achieving that feat in the minds of the Kiowa braves. They knew him by many names and descriptions, but the stories that had probably been created by the Apaches and had spread like a cancer throughout most of the other nomadic tribes referred to him mainly as the dead man who refused to die.

The spirit of a thousand lost souls

could not die because he did not know that he was no longer living. The vivid description of Iron Eyes had seemed far-fetched even to the isolated Kiowa but when they had set eyes on the phantom on horseback, they realized that it was an understatement.

As the Kiowa had watched him from the dense undergrowth they began to believe all the stories they had been fed by their elders around their campfires. It was then they each knew that the tales they had heard were actually true.

Iron Eyes really existed.

Since the logging companies had deemed that it was unprofitable to continue logging in such a remote place and abandoned the huge forest, most people had considered the tree-covered hills devoid of life apart from bears and mountain lions. Yet nothing could have been further from the truth. Several hundred of what was left of the famed Kiowa people had travelled north from their ancestral homeland and replaced the loggers in the wilderness. Yet unlike the long-departed lumberjacks, the Kiowa did not cut down swaths of trees for money.

They had blended into the terrain unnoticed.

As untold numbers of wagon trains had ventured deeper into Kiowa territory, looking for greener pastures and their own brand of paradise, the Indians had deserted what had become known as the Kiowa trail and found a more peaceful place to try and exist. The forested mountains offered them a second chance at surviving amid the relentless onslaught of invaders and they had grasped it.

They knew only too well that this might be their last chance. The secluded mountainous region had provided them with a place where they could live peacefully unhindered by the continuous onslaught of thousands of settlers.

Until the sun had risen that very morning, few men had travelled through the forest due to its remoteness. Those that did venture up into the wilderness had no inkling that the thousands of acres of trees which flanked them had become the adopted home of the Kiowa.

Yet all that suddenly changed when they had spotted Iron Eyes, for unlike other travellers who entered the remote hills, they could not ignore his presence.

It was said that the gaunt bounty hunter was the enemy of all native tribes. Tales of his mindless bloodlust and brutal slayings of untold numbers of Indians were rife in the stories which the twelve Kiowa had been weaned upon.

In truth Iron Eyes had rarely killed anyone if they were not wanted dead or alive. There was no profit in it. Yet the stories had fuelled countless warriors to try their luck and attack him anyway over the years.

It had become a mark of honour.

A lethal ritual built upon a sandy foundation.

The braves would normally have remained secreted and chosen to allow the stranger safe passage rather than risk drawing attention to themselves, but they had soon realized that there was something eerily familiar about the horseman upon the golden stallion.

When they became convinced that the lean emaciated man with long black hair was Iron Eyes, they knew that they could not ignore him.

They believed that the bounty hunter had the blood of countless Indians on his bony hands. This atrocity had to be avenged even if it cost them their own lives.

As with all senseless wars, however large or small, honour and revenge was the vital spark which ignited its fuse and set off a chain reaction that often could not be halted until it was far too late. Just like so many other tribes, the Kiowa had been fed a staple diet of grotesque exaggeration concerning Iron Eyes around their campfires.

With every telling, the tales grew taller and further from the truth. What every tribe failed to understand was that the strange bounty hunter was also hated by white men.

In the eyes of most men, Iron Eyes was neither white nor was he an Indian of any recognizable tribe. His hair was long and black and hung across his wide shoulders just as their hair did. Yet his unholy features did not resemble any known Indian. He was a misfit, a creature that did not belong in either camp, and his mutilated features only added to his misfortune. For men of all colours tend to fear and kill anything which is different to themselves.

The legend that had grown around the fearsome bounty hunter bore no relation to the facts and all most Indians knew about him was that Iron Eyes was said to be a living ghost.

He was a monstrous mistake that could only be fixed by extinction. Just like so many others, the Kiowa believed that he was an evil spirit that they had to try and destroy before he destroyed them.

The twelve highly-painted horsemen

used their unequalled knowledge of the tree-covered hills to not only remain level with the large palomino stallion but to get ahead of it.

Iron Eyes did not know it, but once again he was being stalked by yet another band of highly-skilled hunters. Just like the Apache, Cheyenne and numerous other tribes before them, the Kiowa had decided to undertake the impossible task of claiming the scalp of the man who it was said could never be killed.

The Kiowa hunting party had decided to forget the forest deer they had been tracking and concentrated on a very different game.

Iron Eyes was a prize that they simply could not turn their backs upon. Although they realized that to face the infamous bounty hunter was to face death itself, none of the twelve horsemen could do anything but succumb to the promise of immortality it offered.

The warriors knew that killing Iron Eyes was more than just claiming the scalp of an ordinary white man. Killing

Iron Eyes would make them legends not only amongst their fellow Indians but also in the hearts of the hated white intruders who had driven them from their ancestral homes.

The Kiowa used every shadow at their disposal.

As the powerful stallion obeyed its master's spurs, the warriors tracked its every stride upon their unshod ponies through the trees.

Iron Eyes had only one thought on his mind and that was to find Squirrel Sally and force her back to civilization while there was still time.

Yet as the palomino stretched its sturdy legs and ate up the ground beneath its horseshoes, time was swiftly running out.

The horrific Iron Eyes pressed on at pace.

8

Deep in the heart of the untamed forest several abandoned log cabins remained standing long after the loggers had gone. Most of them had fallen victim to the elements and were uninhabitable but one had somehow managed to withstand the severe seasons and had been found by the three outlaws known simply as the Denver gang.

Jody Denver, Dan Vance and Bill McGee had ridden a long way from their last brutal job back in Senora. There had been six of them when they had ridden into the prosperous cattle town with their eye on the town's bank. Only Denver, McGee and Vance had managed to survive intact after the shooting had stopped.

Jody Denver had always prided himself on his careful planning and yet the robbery had gone badly wrong. To lose three men was bad enough, but also to lose half the loot they had managed to take from the bank's vault was even worse.

As the town barricaded the streets leading to and from the bank, Denver had decided to teach Senora a lesson. It was a brutal and bloody lesson which saw his gang shoot and kill men, women and children with merciless wrath.

The townsfolk had naïvely thought they had managed to thwart the gang by bottling them up but Jody Denver and his followers were not so easily stopped.

They had been like three rattlers in a sack. The smell of freedom was enough for them to show their fangs and spit their venom. They had used practically every gun and rifle bullet to achieve their goal and escape from the barricaded streets of Senora.

As the three surviving outlaws had spurred their way out of the cattle town, more than fifty people lay either dead or wounded. The dry street sand was stained crimson by the blood that was spilled as Denver led McGee and Vance to safety.

There was no posse willing or able to follow the bank robbers as they fled. Senora had learned the hard way that it did not pay to lock horns with outlaws who would rather die than be taken alive.

The Denver gang had kept riding until they discovered the vast wooded hills and the perfect place in which to hold out until they were ready to resume their lethal activities. Jody Denver had expertly guided his gang into the depths of the abandoned logging area and located a shelter.

This was a perfect hideout, or at least it would have been if not for the strange sound that had caught all three men's attention. There was no mistaking the sound of a stagecoach as it rattled along the stone hard trail road. Its powerful six-horse team fighting against the chains which kept them secured between the traces could not be mistaken for any-thing else.

Jody Denver was standing before the log cabin rubbing his neck thoughtfully as McGee and Vance returned with rabbits for the pot slung over their shoulders.

The pair of younger outlaws recognized the expression on Denver's rugged face. The veteran bank robber could not hide his concern from the two men who had ridden with him for over eighteen months.

'What's wrong, Jody?' Vance asked as he dropped the game on to the ground and rubbed the sweat from his temple. 'You look like you seen a ghost.'

Denver glanced briefly at Vance and said nothing as McGee exhaled and dropped his own catch on top of the others. He looked at Denver and then turned and squinted into the dense trees to where the older man was staring.

'What in tarnation are you looking at, Jody?' he asked before squatting on a tree stump. He placed his rifle down beside him. 'There ain't nothing out here except critters.'

Vance moved to the side of Denver, 'What you seen? I reckon I heard me a mountain lion last night. Is that what's chewing at your craw? Have you seen a mountain lion?'

Denver turned on his heels and strode to the cabin. He reached inside and then produced his gun belt. He swung it around his lean girth and buckled it up.

'There's a stagecoach out there someplace, boys.' He announced drily as he pulled his .45 from its holster and checked that it was in full working order.

McGee and Vance looked at one another.

'A stagecoach?' McGee repeated with more than a hint of humour in his tone.

'That's what I said,' Denver flashed his cold eyes at both his men and then thrust the six-shooter back into its holster. 'I heard a stagecoach.'

McGee got back to his feet and tilted his head as his eyes studied the seasoned outlaw. Denver never said anything that he did not firmly believe. 'Are you sure about that, Jody?'

Denver gave a short nod of his head, 'Yep.'

Vance shook his head, 'That's loco talk. What the hell would a stagecoach be doing out here in the middle of nowhere, Jody? That don't make no sense. We ain't on no stagecoach route and this forest is pretty deserted if you ain't noticed.'

Denver stepped away from his men and continued to study the trees. 'I know it don't make any sense but I tell you I heard me a stagecoach.'

Both Vance and McGee looked troubled. They walked to where Denver was standing. Vance placed a hand on the shoulder of the older outlaw.

'Think about it, Jody,' he stammered. 'Nothing ever comes up into these mountains any more. Nothing except varmints like us who want somewhere to rest up and hide for a while.'

'This ain't exactly Wells-Fargo territory, Jody,' McGee shrugged.

Suddenly the noise of pounding hoofs and rattling chains returned to the small

81

clearing around the cabin. It travelled on crisp mountain breeze over the trio of bank robbers.

Denver gave a knowing nod, 'I told you so. If that ain't a stagecoach I'll eat my hat.'

'It sure does sound like a stage, Jody,' McGee admitted.

Vance gulped, 'You're right. That does sound like a stagecoach.'

'Who the hell would be dumb enough to bring a stage up here?' McGee asked out loud. 'That just don't make sense. What the hell is going on?'

'Maybe we should find out,' Denver turned, patted the cheeks of both his men and then grabbed them by their necks. He pulled them toward him and whispered drily. 'Go get your six-guns and then we'll find out who in tarnation is crazy enough to drive around this mountain.'

Vance and McGee ran into the cabin and emerged with their gun belts hanging from their hands. Denver scratched his chin as both men buckled their belts and checked their Peacemakers were loaded.

Vance hesitated, 'Are we leaving the loot unguarded?'

Denver shook his head in frustration, 'Close the cabin door in case a real greedy grizzly decides to rob us, Dan.'

Vance did as he was told and then started to move quickly back to where his cohorts were standing. 'I'm ready.'

'Likewise,' McGee grunted.

Denver pulled the brim of his hat down to shield his eyes and then took a sharp intake of breath. His eyes darted between the men and then he jerked his head at them.

'C'mon, boys,' Denver sighed as his thumb stroked his holstered gun hammer. 'I'm itching to find out who the hell is toying with my head. Some bastard is driving around up on the trail road and I intend finding out who.'

'Ain't we taking the horses, Jody?' Vance asked pointing at their three well-rested mounts tethered to the side of the cabin. 'It wouldn't take long for us to saddle the critters up.'

Denver pointed in the direction of the high trail road. He glanced over his wide shoulder and kept striding toward the trees. 'Where we're going them horses would be more of a liability than a help. Come on.'

The three outlaws continued moving into the undergrowth with their hands resting on their guns. They began to climb the steep tree covered slope.

9

With the haunting sound of the nearby shots still ringing in her ears, Squirrel Sally eased back on the reins and abruptly stopped her muscular team on the precarious slope. The stagecoach rocked on its axle as she pressed her foot against the brake pole. This time the shots had sounded very close, Sally thought.

Too close for comfort.

'That gunplay was way too damn close,' Sally whispered into her cleavage as her small hand cocked the Winchester on her lap in readiness. 'Let 'em come though, I'm eager to kill something right about now. They'll find out soon enough that it don't pay to tangle with Squirrel Sally.'

Her blue eyes glanced through her wavy golden locks and studied the trees like a ravenous mountain lion seeking a glimpse of its next meal. She could hear movement in the ocean of tall pines and then spotted something that surprised her. A thin line of smoke was trailing up from the depths of the forest.

She sniffed the air.

'That sure smells like a campfire to me,' she reasoned before adding. 'Or it might be smoke from a chimney stack.'

Both suggestions did not sit well in the young female's fertile imagination. Sally sucked the last of the tobacco smoke from the pipe and blew it over the backs of her lathered up team.

She pulled the pipe stem from her lips and rested it down beside her thigh. Then she caught the familiar scent of gunsmoke hanging in the crisp mountain air. Its acrid aroma filled her nostrils as she vainly glanced around the area in search of the gun-toting varmint who had fired the unseen weapon.

'I'm getting mighty nervous,' she purred. 'And I'm damn dangerous when I'm nervous.'

Squirrel was more than just nervous.

She was confused but refused to admit it even to herself as she vainly studied the sun-bleached trail road as it wound a route down through the vast trees.

Her heart was beating hard as she wondered who or what she was approaching. For the first time since she had left her family farm to be with her beloved Iron Eyes, she was actually frightened.

Sally could face anything as long as she could see it but whatever was out there in the depths of the forest was hidden from her keen eyes. Like most people who are deprived of a target to focus upon, her imagination was running riot.

The most alarming monsters are created in a terrified imagining. Since time first began the minds of people have always tended to do that.

The team were skittish and fought against their restraints. The chains which held them in check between the traces played a haunting tune as her tiny hands gripped the heavy reins.

Then a troublesome thought filled her heaving bosom.

What if it was Iron Eyes who was being shot at? Had she led him into the gun sights of his enemies? She rubbed the sweat from her temple and then tried to calm herself down. Yet girls cut from the same cloth as young Sally Cooke were not so easily subdued.

She realized if it were the famed bounty hunter on the receiving end of the nerve-chilling gun shots, he might need help.

Her help.

Sally had saved the life of Iron Eyes before. She lifted the hefty long leathers above her head and then thrashed them down across her six-horse team.

The horses immediately sprang into action and started down the steep slope again. This time the urgency burning inside the petite female overshadowed any thoughts of personal safety.

With no fear for her own safety, Sally drove the stagecoach at breakneck speed down the trail road in order to locate Iron Eyes. Every inch of her tiny frame was coming to his aid. Like a mother hen protecting her chick, she was willing to sacrifice her own life for the fearsome bounty hunter.

Sally steered the stagecoach along the severe gradient more masterfully than a full grown man. Her determination outweighed her small stature. The powerful team of matched horses galloped between the traces in blind obedience to her driving skill.

Then as she reached a stretch of level ground, more shots rang out to her right. This time she could see the bullets as they cut through the bushes and ripped branches from the pines.

The fragrant scent of resin drifted on the air as the branches fell in front of the horses. Sally did not know whether to stop or use her bullwhip and race away from the area. The six horses cantered as the tiny female squinted through her unruly golden locks.

Then as the echoes of the gunshots faded into memory she relaxed for a brief moment. She allowed the team to keep trotting as her keen eyes searched for any sign of Iron Eyes or anyone else that might have fired their guns.

Twenty yards ahead of her lead horse, she caught a glimpse of shadows. They were the shadows of at least three men close to the edge of the trail road. She pulled back on her long leathers and pressed her foot against the brake pole.

The stagecoach stopped.

She looped the reins around the pole and then picked up her Winchester and held it against her exposed flesh. She had heard their gunshots and seen their shadows but no matter how hard her eyes strained, she could not see the men themselves.

Sally licked her lips and then with the rifle gripped in her hands she rose and stepped up on to the roof of the coach and moved hurriedly toward the rear of the stationary vehicle.

Sally slid down the tarp covering the trunk of the stagecoach and landed on the ground. She crouched with her trusty carbine in her hands and looked under the body of the coach. Her eyes narrowed as they looked beyond the legs of the six horses but she still could not see the three men whose shadows she had seen on the road.

Sally bit her lip and slowly straightened up. She looked to both sides of the trail. She knew exactly where she had caught a glimpse of the shadows.

Then out of the blue a gunshot rang out. A bullet hit the back of the coach trunk sending hot splinters into the air. The small female swung on the balls of her feet and was about to dash for the almost black undergrowth when another shot rang out.

This time the lead came closer.

She ducked as more wood was carved out from the rear of the stagecoach. As she crouched near the ground her eyes darted to both sides of the trail. Whoever was firing at her was well hidden, she thought.

Then she heard boots. She looked along the length of the vehicle's belly and saw the legs of a man heading directly at her lead horses.

'Damn it all,' she cursed. 'I'm sure in a pickle and no mistake.'

As she rested on one knee wishing that she had a clear shot at the advancing man, she heard the unmistakable sound of a gun hammer being cocked behind her. She went to turn when another gun hammer was cocked. Sally raised her head and was staring straight into the smoking barrel of Bill McGee's .45.

She blew the long curls off her face.

'Drop the rifle, missy,' Vance growled from behind her.

Sally gritted her teeth. Every inch of her crouched form wanted to rise and start shooting at the men who were coming at her from three different sides just as her beloved Iron Eyes would have done. But Sally was all too aware that she was not the lethal bounty hunter and would never get away with it.

Her small hands reluctantly released the rifle and allowed it to slide to the ground. Only then did she rise and rest her knuckles on her shapely hips.

As Jody Denver walked to the rear of the stagecoach to join his two companions, his expression suddenly altered at the sight before him. His eyebrows rose up into his furrowed temple as a lustful smile filled his whiskered face.

'Now what have we here?' he sighed.

Sally raised her head and glared through her entangled golden hair at the leader of the Denver gang. Her defiant eyes darted between all three of the outlaws as they each drooled at her.

'You best not be getting any notions, boys,' she warned them before carefully pulling the tails of her weathered shirt together and tying them in a knot over her belly button. 'My man is coming looking for me and he don't cotton to horn-toads.'

Denver grunted with amusement as he pondered her carefully. 'Just who is your man, beautiful?'

'Iron Eyes,' Sally snarled.

Both Vance and McGee looked at Denver. His expression had changed just as theirs had done. Every scrap of lust had evaporated into the afternoon sun from the gang leader's face.

Before either of his men could start talking, Denver silenced them with a wave of his hand. He stepped closer to the petite Sally and looked down on her fearless face.

'How'd you know Iron Eyes?' he growled.

'I'm Squirrel Sall. I'm his woman,' Sally boasted. 'Now let me go and we'll forget about this.'

Denver grabbed her mane of golden curls and violently raised it high so that her feet were barely touching the ground. As her clenched fists vainly tried to punch the veteran outlaw, Denver glared into her fiery eyes.

'There ain't no way that we can let you go, girl,' he snarled at her. 'You just told us that Iron Eyes is coming looking for you. When that stinking bounty hunter hears about me and the boys, he'll come looking for us.'

Dangling like a fresh caught fish, Sally looked into the outlaw's eyes. She was puzzled.

'I don't understand,' she blurted out. 'Why would Iron Eyes come looking for you?'

'We're wanted dead or alive, honey-child,' Denver said before throwing her into the arms of his two companions. 'I've heard that your man would crawl over hot coals to get his hands on bounty.'

Sally's expression suddenly changed as the reality of her situation suddenly dawned upon her. She did not notice the wandering hands of the two outlaws who groped her. All she could do was stare at Denver in a bewilderment.

'What you figuring on doing?' she shouted feverishly at him. 'Tell me.'

'That's plumb simple,' Denver stooped, plucked her prized Winchester up off the ground and then turned. He paused and glared at the tiny tornado. 'We can't afford to have you take this stagecoach down the hill and let you tell Iron Eyes that you just bumped into three wanted outlaws, gal. The safest thing is for us to haul you back to our cabin and wait there for him to show up.'

Squirrel Sally wrestled against the two younger outlaws who held her in check but her entire attention was on the thoughtful Denver as he looked around the area.

'It ain't gonna work,' she yelled furiously at Denver as she wriggled and kicked at the men restraining her. 'Iron Eyes ain't dumb enough to ride into your trap.'

Denver eyed her up and down. The bright sunlight danced upon her sweating figure. He shrugged and started to head back to their isolated refuge. 'I sure would if I was Iron Eyes and you were the bait, gal.'

10

The massive well-nourished branches hung from both sides of the trail as the bounty hunter drew back on his reins and stopped the flagging stallion. A cloud of dust rose from around its hoofs and filtered into the blistering sunlight. Iron Eyes rubbed the grime from his horrific features and then looked all around him in search of anything that might give him a clue as to where the young Sally might be. The sound of the shots was now a distant memory but the gaunt horseman could not relax.

There was something haunting about this wilderness. He had travelled through many forests during his life as a hunter, but there was something different about this one. Yet no matter how much he dwelled upon it, he could not find any answers to the questions that continued to haunt him.

Iron Eyes was close to exhaustion and that hindered his ability to reason. In the hours since he had killed the back-shooting bounty hunters he had sensed that there was far more danger hidden within the confines of this forest.

A well-rested Iron Eyes would have noticed the way the wildlife within the forest reacted as he rode ever onward in his quest to locate Squirrel, but he was dog-tired.

There was only so far that a man, even Iron Eyes, could go without stopping to consume anything more nourishing than whiskey and cigar smoke. Had he been more alert he would have realized that he was being followed by the unseen Kiowa.

As the curious warriors watched from the undergrowth, Iron Eyes only knew that the countless trees could have an army hidden behind their wide tree trunks and no one would be any the wiser.

Iron Eyes looked at the savage wound on his shoulder. His bony digits peeled back the torn fabric of his coat and looked upon his injury. Blood still trailed from the inch-square chunk of his missing flesh, but there was no time to tend the wound. His stamina was waning as he fumbled among his bullet-filled pockets until he located another twisted cigar. He placed it between his razor sharp teeth and then produced a match and struck it on his silver saddlehorn. He filled his lungs and then slowly exhaled. The smoke eased the pain as he tossed the spent match at the ground.

He knew that Sally was pig-headed enough to keep on travelling until he caught up with her. That was exactly what she was doing. The trouble was she had no idea where she was going or what dangers she might be drawing to her the way flies get dragged to an outhouse short on fresh lime.

Squirrel had him hooked like a prize pike and he was being reeled in whether he liked it or not. Like a tempestuous child, the tiny female was stubborn.

'That gal is gonna be the death of me,' he said through smoke as it drifted from his mouth and encircled his weary shoulders. 'By the time I catch up with her I'm gonna be too tuckered to kick her rump.'

His narrowed eyes squinted into the brilliant sun and searched the area intently. The lower trail he had chosen to continue his journey was about a quarter of a mile below the main trail but he figured that they were both headed in the same direction. He had been an easy target on the far wider trail and there had been no cover.

At least this winding route would offer him the cover of countless trees when the shooting started again. Iron Eyes was convinced that it was only a matter of time before another lowlife back-shooter tried his luck and unleashed his bullets in his direction.

He rubbed his red-raw eyes.

The shimmering haze that rose up from the hot sandy trail had confused him at first. He nudged the palomino and allowed his mount to walk another ten strides before stopping the muscular animal again. The trail ahead of the proud stallion snaked off into the distance.

It was shrouded in virtually impenetrable cover. Shafts of dazzling sunlight cut down through gaps in the overhead canopy and shimmered before his burning eyes. The trail road that had been wide a few miles back was now much narrower as nature had started to reclaim it. It was still far wider than his muscular mount though, he thought.

Iron Eyes tapped his spurs.

The palomino began to walk again. As it moved the animal raised its head and sniffed at the forest air and then started to snort. Iron Eyes knew only too well that the stallion could smell water. He allowed the horse to increase its pace as it instinctively headed to where it knew it would find the precious liquid it craved.

As the massive stallion gathered speed, Iron Eyes hung on to the reins and studied the land they were travelling through. Yet the forest was mocking his attempt to see deeper into its entanglement.

Iron Eyes pulled the cigar from his lips and tapped its ash away as the large horse kept moving at speed through the eerie terrain. He then returned the bent cigar to his mouth and tried vainly to relax. It was impossible. No matter how hard he tried, his hunter's gut kept telling him that there was terrible danger in this land. Yet he had not seen any wild animals since first entering the forest. If there were cougars and bears in this wilderness, they were either waiting for sundown or they were far up the tree-covered hills.

As his tortured mind attempted to remain calm, the most dreaded bounty hunter of them all knew that his dwindling instincts sensed a very different type of danger.

The two-legged type of gun-toting hombres who were always ready and willing to start shooting, just like the pair of dead men he had left a few miles behind him.

He hung on to his long leathers as the sturdy mount twisted and turned as it galloped through the encroaching undergrowth. Smoke trailed over his wide shoulders just like the twelve Kiowa who kept pace with him astride their painted ponies.

Then the stallion turned off the trail and forced its way through heavy brush. It had found its goal. The large animal slowed to a walk as it neared the sparkling brook. Even Iron Eyes could smell the crystal clear water as it tumbled relentlessly down a small waterfall and collected in a hollow just ahead of the palomino.

Iron Eyes sucked the last of the smoke from the cigar and then flicked it into the fast moving water as it continued on its way down the mountainside. He looped a long bony leg over the lowered head of the horse and slid off. The ground was soft around the brook as the bounty hunter pulled all of his empty canteens off the horn of his saddle and moved to the edge of the water.

Iron Eyes knelt beside the rippling water. His eyes glanced at the drinking horse and then vainly searched the surrounding area. Although he still could not see anything but trees, he still sensed that death was mighty close. He unscrewed the stoppers of the canteen and then lowered them into the clear water. Bubbles surfaced as the dishevelled bounty hunter patiently waited.

'This ain't a good idea, horse,' he growled. 'Just remember it was your notion to come here, not mine. I'm looking for that gold-stealing little Squirrel. I don't even like the taste of water.'

One by one he filled the canteens and placed them on the muddy ground beside him. Although he had never cared too much for water, he curiously cupped his hands and raised the cold liquid to his mouth. He drank from his hands and then dried his palms on his blood-stained coat front.

A horrified expression nearly out-weighed his normally scarred features as he swallowed. Iron Eyes angrily glanced at the palomino beside him as the stallion continued to consume the precious liquid.

Iron Eyes spat at the mud.

'How in tarnation can you drink this stuff, horse?' he groaned before returning his deathly stare to his surroundings and then grabbing the canteens and standing. He hung each of the ice-cold containers to the ornate silver horn of his saddle before pulling another twisted cigar from his pocket and placing it in his mouth.

Iron Eyes scratched a match with his thumbnail, but before he could raise the flickering flame to the cigar between his teeth he heard something.

There was something about the noise that an arrow makes as it leaves a bow, which once heard, is never forgotten. It was a memory that was branded into every sinew of the tall figure as he momentarily paused. The arrow whistled passed the bounty hunter's ear, lifting his long mane off his blood-stained shoulder.

'Damn it all,' Iron Eyes yelped as he grabbed hold of the horse's loose leathers and threw his lean frame off the ground and on to the Mexican saddle. 'We got company, Gluepot.'

As more deadly projectiles flew at him from the dense forest, Iron Eyes swiftly dragged one of his Navy Colt's from his belt and blasted a reply.

The trees resonated to the deafening sound of the bounty hunter's gun as Iron Eyes fought to control the handsome beast beneath him. Then one of the arrows narrowly missed his leg and embedded into the well-constructed saddle.

'It's getting mighty unhealthy around here,' Iron Eyes drawled and then drove his bloody spurs into the flanks of the confused animal. 'C'mon. Get me out of here.'

With more arrows flying through the air in his direction, the palomino crossed the fast-flowing water and then ploughed through a wall of entangled undergrowth. As the gaunt horseman spurred, he felt his long dust coat almost ripped from his determined body. With blood trailing from a hundred cuts, Iron Eyes forced the stallion forward as his teeth gripped on to the flavoursome weed.

The palomino leapt over a fallen tree

trunk with the agility of an attacking cougar. The muscular animal did not miss a stride as its hoofs landed on the forest floor. Iron Eyes dropped the smoking six-shooter into one of his dust coat pockets and then withdrew its identical twin and cocked its hammer.

Iron Eyes twisted and looked over his shoulder at his unseen attackers. There was no sign of them but he knew they were still there. He could hear their ponies battling with the skin-ripping thorny undergrowth as they pursued him. He swung back around and stared over the creamy mane of the charging stallion.

'Damn it all,' he yelled out as he hung on as best he could. 'I hate Injuns even more than I hate cowboys.'

11

The three outlaws had wrapped one of their pants belts around Squirrel Sally's middle and buckled it so tightly, she could hardly breathe let alone swing her clenched fists which hung at her thighs. The fiery female was angry at herself far more than her captors. This was the first time that anyone had managed to get the better of her and she felt vulnerable. Yet there was no fear in the petite Sally. Her smouldering eyes glared through her golden locks at the men who had virtually quelled any chance of her being able to defend herself. Her time travelling with the infamous Iron Eyes had taught her that there was always an angle to escape even the most deadly of situations.

All you had to do was figure it out.

With every step of her bare feet, Squirrel Sally pondered on the situation she had blundered into. If there was a way out of this, she was confident in finding it.

Sally turned her head and stared at the men who had her penned in. Denver had her prized Winchester in his gloved hands and was toying with the lethal rifle.

'Be careful with that carbine,' she warned as Vance pushed her forward, 'That rifle's got a hair trigger.'

Jody Denver glanced at their attractive captive. 'You ever use this rifle, gal?'

She chuckled. 'I sure have. I've killed me a heap of worthless varmints with that toothpick. I'll kill you with it when I get me the chance.'

Denver laughed and pushed her out into the clearing and toward the small cabin as McGee and Vance flanked the leader of the infamous Denver gang.

'Do you reckon she's telling the truth, Jody?' McGee uneasily asked.

Denver shook his head as they crossed the clearing toward the cabin and their tethered horses. 'Nope, I reckon it's just big talk from a little runt, boys.'

The rage burned inside the small Sally. She fumed and looked ahead as her three captors kept forcing her toward their hideout with the barrels of their weaponry.

'Keep moving, Squirrel Sally,' Denver chuckled as his gun barrel pressed into the small of her back. 'I'm darn grateful you told me who you are. Now all we gotta do is wait for your man to come looking for his sweetheart and kill him. With Iron Eyes out of the way, we won't have nothing to worry about.'

The sudden realization that she was the lure which would get her beloved Iron Eyes killed dawned on her. Her beautiful blue eyes flashed behind the cover of her golden mane as she desperately tried to struggle from the leather belt that kept her arms glued to her hips and thighs.

'Why'd you wanna kill Iron Eyes for?' she yelled.

Denver looked down at her, 'Simple. He's the most feared bounty hunter there is. Killing him will free us up to get back to work. Iron Eyes is the most dangerous of his stinking breed and once he's dead we ain't got nothing to trouble us.'

Denver's words chilled Sally.

'He'll kill you all before you got time to spit,' Sally snarled like a trapped animal as they neared the cabin. She glanced up at the shingled roof and the stove smoke which billowed from its chimney. 'Iron Eyes ain't so easily killed and once he's riled, he'll show you no mercy'

All three outlaws laughed in amusement at her stammering outburst. They had all heard of the notorious bounty hunter's reputation but none of the trio could imagine how dangerous he truly was.

'You'll find out who the best guns are, missy,' Vance pushed her hard. Sally stumbled and fell heavily on to the ground close to their tethered mounts. The animals shied and snorted as she rolled up to their hoofs. 'If'n you weren't so pretty, I'd put a bullet in you now.'

Denver placed Sally's rifle against the cabin wall and stared down at his attractive prisoner. 'We're the Denver gang, gal. We're wanted in places that we ain't even heard of and we kill anyone who gets in our way.'

Sally blew a stray ringlet of hair off her face and stared up at the trio of deadly bank-robbers. Her youthful mind raced as she concentrated on them, seeking a chink in their armour.

'So you're the Denver gang?' she asked as she swung around on her buttocks and sighed heavily. 'I heard about you boys but I never thought you were yellow-bellies.'

Rage erupted in the soul of McGee. He went to lash out with his boot when Denver pulled him back. Both men stared at one another for a few moments.

'That gal talks too much, Jody,' McGee grunted, pointing his six-gun in her defiant direction.

Denver gave a slow nod of his head.

'I know she does, but don't go falling for her big talk. She's just a scared runt who uses her mouth to fend off her enemies, Bill.'

McGee glared down at the seated female and pointed a shaking finger at her, 'Why'd you call us yellow-bellies?'

Sally looked around the remote area and then back at the furious outlaw.

'Why? Only a bunch of cowards hide in the middle of a forest,' she grinned. 'Real men would face their enemies. They sure wouldn't hide out like vermin.'

Vance circled both his cohorts without taking his eyes from the seated young vixen they had brought to their stronghold. He paused and stared down at her sun-kissed body barely contained by her ripped and weathered clothing. He licked his lips as though he was studying a freshly baked pie and then shook his head before looking to his companions.

'She sure is mighty juicy, boys,' he noted. 'I'm gonna enjoy teaching her about the birds and bees.'

Sally's eyes darted up at the grinning man, 'Keep on drooling, fathead. It'll be the death of you.'

'She sure is sassy,' Vance gave out a belly laugh and grabbed her long hair. He lifted it away from her body and admired her well-developed womanhood. 'I bet you're a real tiger when an hombre pays you some interest.'

'Leave her be, Dan,' Denver said as he moved toward their captive and looked down upon the seductive Sally. 'If anyone is gonna taste how sweet she is, it's me.'

'How come?' Vance grunted.

'This is my gang, Dan,' Denver reminded the far younger outlaw like a stag marking its territory. 'I always get first bite of the apple and don't you ever forget it. You can have my left-overs.'

Vance silently snorted and sat on a tree stump. He continued to glare at Sally like a starving man confronted by a mouth-watering feast.

Sally rested her head on her raised knees. From the corner of her eye she could see the sun glinting off her trusty rifle propped against the cabin wall.

McGee looked long and hard at Sally before turning his eyes to Denver. 'She sure is a fiery little gal, Jody. Reckon she bites?'

Denver laughed and moved to his Winchester, which was lying beside their other weaponry on a crude table just inside the cabin. He lifted it and cranked its hand-guard. 'I'd bet a hundred bucks that she bites and uses her claws as well.'

'I like feisty gals,' McGee winked.

Denver began loading his rifle and watched their prisoner with seasoned eyes as she sat in the dust. 'Look at her, Bill. She ain't no taller than a kid but she's smart. That gal is like a wild animal and there ain't nothing more fearsome than a wild animal. Give her half a chance and she'd slit your throat or rip out your eyes.'

McGee swallowed hard as he rested his hand on his holstered gun. Sweat trailed down his face as he looked at the seated female as she stared at the sun-baked soil between her bare feet.

'Are you serious?' he whispered out of the corner of his mouth at Denver. 'You really figure she's that wild?'

Denver briefly glanced at Sally before returning to his rifle, 'Yep, I reckon. What other kind of female would ride with the likes of Iron Eyes?'

McGee rubbed his throat, 'Holy smoke. I never considered that. You're right, Jody. Iron Eyes would only tangle with a gal as mean as he is. She sure is pretty though.'

Denver nodded in agreement, 'They're the worst kind. The pretty ones are always the worst of the bunch. Just think on the whores in all the saloons you've bin in, Bill. The prettier they are, the more unpredictable they are. The ugly ones are always a whole heap safer.'

McGee moved across the cabin and fed the stove with logs before placing the coffee pot on its flat surface. He chewed on the words of his elder before returning to the man who was ensuring all their rifles were fully loaded.

'Even so,' he shrugged. 'I'd still like to have me a crack at that young filly, Jody.'

'You can. When I'm through with that gal,' Denver drawled, 'You and Dan are welcome to what's left, Bill.'

McGee grinned, 'I'll rustle up some grub, Jody.'

Denver nodded and placed the fully-loaded rifle next to the others. He rested a broad shoulder against the door frame and then looked around the clearing.

'If that little gal is telling the truth,' he started. 'Iron Eyes will be here pretty soon looking for his frisky little Squir-rel.'

Sweat dripped from the young out-law's face as he anxiously looked across the cabin at Denver.

'I ain't in no hurry to tangle with that critter,' McGee admitted as he placed the blackened skillet on the stove top.

Denver gave a terrifying grin. 'I am.'

12

After riding for what felt like an eternity, Iron Eyes finally drew back on his long leathers and hauled the powerful palomino to a stop. The snorting stallion was sweating heavily as its master slid from its saddle and rested his back against its coiled saddle rope. His bony hand pulled the arrow from the heavily padded Mexican saddle.

His narrowed eyes studied the arrow carefully. He traced a finger along the wooden shaft and then stared at the feathered flights. Every tribe could be identified by the tell-tale feathers they emblazoned their arrows with, but the wounded bounty hunter had never encountered any Indian who used this exact type of flight.

The arrow had come within inches of his leg. Iron Eyes angrily snapped the shaft in half and tossed it aside.

'What tribe have I upset this time, horse?' he drawled as the stallion started to chew on the plentiful vegetation surrounding them. 'I don't recognize them flights at all. We're too far north for it to be Apaches and it sure ain't Cheyenne or Sioux. Whoever they are, they're just like all the others and don't like me.'

His eyes looked from behind the veil of long black strands of hair that dangled limply over his hideous face. The famed bounty hunter did not trust anything in this strange land of innumerable trees. His wound hurt like hell and was throbbing constantly under the tattered fabric of his dust coat. He flexed his long bony fingers and shook his hand in an attempt to stop his tendons from seizing up.

'Where the hell is Squirrel?' Iron Eyes hissed at his resting horse. 'Trying to catch up with that little vixen is proving more dangerous than tracking outlaws.'

The wounded bounty hunter paced around the stallion as his weary mind raced. He had no idea where Sally's trail had led him to or what sort of

Indians might haunt this forest.

His ignorance troubled him as he checked the satchels to both sides of the tall animal. He lifted the last bottle of whiskey from the saddlebags and pulled its cork with his skeletal fingers and then raised it to his lips. He washed the taste of anger down his gullet and then exhaled heavily.

He glanced at the sky and then returned his attention back to the faithful palomino. The handsome horse was starting to look as beleaguered as its master.

'I sure hope Squirrel had the sense to buy some whiskey with some of my money, horse,' he drawled as the fumes filled his head and cleared his thoughts. Then another less savoury thought came to the bounty hunter. 'Whatever tribe was taking pot shots at me might have also taken a hankering to her long golden hair. I'd sure not like for her to get scalped.'

Iron Eyes dried his lips along his sleeve. He rubbed his chin as the notion of Sally's scalp hanging from an Indian's lance chilled him to the bone.

A fresh sense of urgency filled his pitifully lean frame as he began to picture the horrific scene of the stubborn Sally's hair as nothing more than a trophy. Iron Eyes shuddered and then glanced at his shoulder again.

Crimson gore still seeped from the hole in his shoulder and he knew that he had to stop any more blood from escaping his frame. His eyes darted around the forest and then spotted a sun-drenched fallen tree trunk a few yards to his right. His long legs strode to the trunk. He pressed his hand against its moss-filled interior. It was bone dry unlike most of the forest, he thought. A gap in the overhead canopy allowed a steady flood of sunlight to warm the ground in a twenty-foot radius of the fallen tree.

'Reckon I got enough time to tend this blasted wound,' he muttered to himself as he scooped more leaves on to the moss and patted them down. 'This oughta do just fine.'

Iron Eyes pulled out his long bladed Bowie knife from the neck of his mule-eared boot and forced its blade into the dry moss. He took another swig of whiskey and then located a match and ignited it with his thumbnail. He dropped the match on to the moss and then spat the fiery liquor on to the moss. A flash of explosive heat hit the bounty hunter. Within seconds the entire interior of the rotten tree trunk was ablaze around his trusty knife.

His narrowed eyes stared at the bone handle of his lethal knife as flames licked around its honed blade. A sultry smile etched the corner of his scarred face. His bony finger pushed the knife sending scarlet whispers upward toward the branches that loomed high above the skeletal figure.

All the bounty hunter could now do was wait. Wait for the Bowie knife to get good and hot. His keen hearing listened out for any telltale sign that the Kiowa were drawing closer.

'So far so good,' Iron Eyes muttered as he carefully placed the whiskey bottle down on the ground beside his mule-eared boots. He tilted his head. His limp black hair fell over his gruesome face as he watched the cold steel grow redder in the burning innards of the trunk.

Every few seconds he placed more kindling on the fire and then peeled his jacket and shirt off his shoulder. A scarlet stream of bloody droplets wept and oozed from the flesh.

Iron Eyes twisted his tortured head as the sound of approaching ponies caught his grim attention. The bounty hunter knew that his adversaries had discovered his trail again and were now only minutes from the small clearing.

He turned back to the fire and tore a strip off his shirt and wrapped it around his bony hand.

'I sure hope them Injuns keep their distance for a while,' he muttered as he felt the heat of the fire against his brutalized flesh. 'I gotta fix this wound fast before them Injuns figure out where I am.'

His bony hand gripped the bone handle of the knife and poked the fire. A million red hot sparks rose up into the eerie forest. He knew that this was going to hurt like sin. It always hurt like sin.

Iron Eyes swallowed hard and then drew the blade from the fire and swiftly laid it across the savage wound. Sizzling skin hissed from the melted skin. Pain raced through his emaciated body like a lightning bolt. The knife fell from his hand as the bounty hunter buckled.

With the sickening smell of burning flesh filling his flared nostrils, his shaking hand grabbed the whiskey bottle and raised it to his scarred lips.

He filled his mouth with whiskey and then turned his head and stared at the smoking wound. Iron Eyes spat a steady stream of whiskey on to the wound and then swayed as he fought with the desire to succumb to unconsciousness.

Iron Eyes returned the bottle neck to

his mouth and started to drain its contents. The whiskey tasted good as it forged a trail into his guts. As the last drop of the fiery liquid drained from the bottle, Iron Eyes rubbed the beads of sweat from his brow, tossed the bottle aside and then plucked the knife off the ground. He returned the blackened blade to his boot, then forced himself back up to his full height.

Most men who had just endured the pain which the notorious bounty hunter had inflicted upon himself to quell any further loss of blood would have keeled over, but not Iron Eyes. The gaunt figure had a keen sense of self-preservation burning through him. It was far hotter than the blade that he had used to stem the incessant blood flow.

Iron Eyes staggered back to the palomino, grabbed his reins and then slowly mounted the sturdy stallion. As the bounty hunter gathered his wits as well as the long leathers, his attention was drawn to a noise behind his wide back.

A flurry of arrows peppered the ground around the stallion as Iron Eyes gripped his reins tightly. His icy stare glanced over his blood soaked shoulder at the brightly painted warriors as they drove their ponies toward the clearing. The Kiowa had seen the smoke rising up into the sky and were charging through the trees at him. They unleashed more lethal projectiles at the bounty hunter.

'I sure hate wasting bullets on critters that ain't got bounty on their heads,' he snarled. Fearlessly, Iron Eyes pulled one of his six-shooters from his pants belt and quickly fired three shots in quick succession at the howling warriors before swinging the powerful stallion around and spurring.

The chilling sound of their whooping had not frightened the bounty hunter, but had instantly brought him out of his delirium. Iron Eyes gritted his razor-sharp teeth and forced the stallion on at a breakneck speed.

The wide-eyed palomino jumped over the blazing tree trunk and accelerated along the gully. Its pounding hoofs raced through the forest as its painfully lean master hung on and continued firing back at his relentless pursuers.

Yet the potentially lethal bullets did not slow the warriors as they charged across the clearing. The ponies leapt through the flames of the blazing tree trunk in determined pursuit. Iron Eyes fired the last of his six-shooters bullets and then swapped weapons as he steered the palomino down through the brush. Even as his bony hand cocked and fired back at the howling warriors, they kept on coming.

Not even the possibility of death could slow their progress. The Kiowa steered their slightly built ponies after the haunting figure who continued to evade their arrows.

The chase had become something far more than just wanting to kill an intruder. Now it was a quest to finally put an end to the legendary Iron Eyes. To do what so many other Indians had failed to do.

They were determined to destroy the mythical creature that had fuelled their nightmares for so long. They wanted to slay the hideous Iron Eyes and hold his freshly scalped mane of black hair aloft for all to see. To prove the sheer might of the Kiowa. To prove that even mythical monsters could be hunted and vanquished like all other beings.

As the golden stallion obeyed its master's spurs, arrows lifted his coat tails. Iron Eyes mercilessly whipped the stallion with the ends of his reins and fired his Navy Colt in a futile bid to halt the Indians who just would not quit.

The palomino thundered through the undergrowth and headed deeper into the black heart of the forest hills. The thick overhead branches prevented the blistering sun from penetrating this section of the forest yet the Kiowa were still hot on his tail.

Their howls gnawed at his very marrow. The bounty hunter had managed to put distance between himself and the Kiowa but knew that their smaller ponies were far more agile in this rough terrain. Iron Eyes realized that he had to find high ground quickly if he were going to get the better of determined Kiowa braves.

Iron Eyes had to summon every trick he had learned over the years if he were going to have a chance of escaping the wrath of his pursuers. His eyes darted from behind his limp strands of hair as they searched for a way out of this perilous situation.

His bony hands pulled hard on his leathers and turned the galloping animal sharply. Like a man possessed, he rode between the tall straight trees narrowly avoiding their low hanging branches and then turned the palomino yet again.

The snorting stallion nearly fell as its hoofs battled with the muddy ground beneath his hoofs. Somehow the muscular horse righted itself and gasped for air as its master studied the treacherous terrain again.

Iron Eyes ducked as an arrow flew past his face, then swung the horse around and whipped his long leathers again. The palomino obeyed and charged.

The bounty hunter's narrowed eyes spotted a steep muddy slope rising up from the floor of the gully to higher ground. It was about two hundred yards to his right beyond the entangled trees and undergrowth. Iron Eyes sensed that if he were to escape the deadly arrows of his attackers, the steep muddy slope might be his only option.

Not wishing his followers to realize his intention, he rode parallel with the imposing slope. His mind raced as the nerve-rattling sound of the Kiowa grew more intense behind him. With arrows flying all around him, Iron Eyes glanced at the steep slope again and continued to force his mount to weave in and out of the trees.

It appeared impossible to ascend but the wounded bounty hunter had never been easily deterred. To Iron Eyes the impossible was merely a challenge not yet tackled.

The gaunt horseman turned his mount

again. He spurred and crashed through a wall of thorny brush and then cracked his reins across the muscular horse's creamy tail.

'C'mon, horse,' he yelled out and blasted one of his trusty Navy Colt's at the trailing warriors. 'We'll make them Injuns wish they'd never set eyes on either of us.'

Iron Eyes had tried everything to shake his pursuers off his trail but they were still chasing him. The noise of their arrows embedding into trees chilled the fearsome rider as his keen eyes vainly searched for another way to escape their wrath.

No matter where Iron Eyes cast his attention, there was no other option but the muddy incline. The daunting slope was damp with moisture and covered in spindly trees but it was the only way out of the corner he had ridden into. The howling Kiowa had somehow managed to drive him into a place where there was no hope of escape.

Yet their prey was no ordinary man, just as his mount was no ordinary horse. Neither accepted defeat as a meal they could or would chew on. Iron Eyes gritted his teeth and stared angrily at the slope. It loomed over both horse and rider like a mythical dragon the bounty hunter vowed to slay.

Iron Eyes pushed his gun into his dust coat pocket and stared at the slippery slope again. Every atom of his emaciated body began to hate the muddy obstacle as though it were a living creature. A creature he wanted to defeat far more than the whooping Kiowa.

He hauled back on his reins then twisted in his saddle and started to ride through a maze of sturdy fir trees. Iron Eyes was trying to mislead the band of warriors to which way he was heading. Yet with every stride the tall palomino took as it used the trees as a shield, Iron Eyes' icy stare kept returning to the steep slope.

Iron Eyes knew that nobody in their right mind would even attempt to try and ride a horse up the muddy incline, but that made it all the more appealing to the wounded man. As he lashed the ends of his long leathers back and forth across the shoulders of the golden stallion, Iron Eyes reasoned that the Indians would never believe that he was actually going to attempt the impossible.

A twisted grin carved across his mutilated face.

Apart from the thin trees dotted across the side of the slope all the bounty hunter could see was mud. Mud the colour of spilled gore. He slapped the neck of his trusty horse and then headed straight at the severe incline.

'C'mon, horse,' he bellowed. 'You can do it.'

The powerful stallion jinked between trees, jumped over boulders and countless fallen trees which were scattered across the floor of the forest as it instantly responded to its master's growls. The magnificent palomino defied its weariness and charged like a raging bull at the wall of mud.

The deathly horseman stood in his stirrups, leaned over the shoulders of the palomino as another volley of lethal arrows narrowly missed his pitifully lean frame. Iron Eyes knew the horse needed to build up momentum if it were going to climb the scarlet slope. Another arrow clipped his mane of flapping hair as it passed within inches of his face.

It only made Iron Eyes more determined.

The arrows were getting too close, he thought. Too damn close for comfort. Iron Eyes whipped the horse's shoulders feverishly as the muscular animal hurtled toward the wall of mud.

'Fly, horse,' He yelled. 'Fly like you got wings.'

13

The echoing sound of Iron Eyes' distant gunfire drifted on the mountain breeze and washed over Jody Denver and his trusty cohorts. For the first time since they had captured Squirrel Sally they began to actually believe the petite female had been telling them the truth. The infamous bounty hunter was close and getting closer by the sound of it.

'You figure that's Iron Eyes, Jody?' Vance asked nervously.

'I guess so,' Denver replied dryly as his rubbed the knuckle of his thumb against his jawbone. He glanced at the female who was still on her backside.

'He'll kill the whole bunch of you critters when he gets here, boys,' Sally smiled. 'Then he'll haul your carcasses to the closest town and collect the bounty on your heads.'

More shots rang out from the depths

of the ocean of trees and hung in the mountain air. The three outlaws glanced at one another. They knew that the tiny young Sally was probably telling them what would surely happen if they did not stop the infamous bounty hunter.

Denver looked around the area as the sun finally dropped below the tall trees. Night was quickly approaching and by the sound of the gunshots, so was the feared Iron Eyes. The veteran outlaw rubbed his unshaven jaw as he turned to Vance and McGee.

'It's time to set the trap,' Denver said anxiously before pointing at Sally. 'Get this little runt into the cabin right now.'

Vance and McGee walked toward the seated Sally.

They grabbed an arm each and lifted Squirrel Sally off the ground. They carried her kicking and shouting form into the small structure and threw her into a cabin corner. As she skidded on her britches her eyes narrowed and glared through her dangling locks at the trio of deadly outlaws.

Sally winced as she lifted each buttock in turn off the unforgiving boards to relieve the stinging. Then she lifted her head and yelled at the top of her voice at them.

'You stinking bastards,' Sally yelped as she felt splinters filling her rear. 'If my hands were free I'd send you all to Hell. You ain't nothing but cowards. Snot-nosed cowards.'

All three of the outlaws chuckled as her words filled the confines of the log cabin. Sally quickly glanced around its interior and made a mental note of its layout. She noted that it had just one door and a solitary window. There was no glass in the window frame and its shutters were wide open to the elements. Her fertile imagination raced as she tried to figure out how to escape from the three brutal captors. Her mind kept returning to thought of her fully loaded Winchester propped against the outside wall of the cabin.

If she could just free herself and reach the rifle, everything would change.

Denver checked that the belt wrapped around Sally's arms was still secure. He then tightened it a notch under her heaving breasts. A wry smile etched his hardened features as he licked lips at the sight of her sweat soaked flesh.

'I'm gonna enjoy servicing you, Squirrel,' he drooled, touching her chin.

'I'm gonna enjoy killing you,' Sally retorted.

Denver straightened up, rested his knuckles on his hips and grinned down at the young beauty as she vainly wriggled in an attempt to free herself.

'That should keep you under control,' Denver said.

Sally glanced at the senior outlaw and spat. 'You'll find out how hard it is to keep me under control, old timer.'

Denver shook his fist at her.

'Now shut that big mouth of yours, gal,' Denver shouted at her as he and his cohorts prepared for the coming of night and the potential arrival of the infamous bounty hunter. 'I'm curious as to whether you've bin telling us the truth about you being Iron Eyes' woman.'

Sally's eyebrows arched, 'You calling me a liar?'

'If the shoe fits,' Denver snarled.

'Shoe? What shoe?' Sally yelled as she stared at her bare feet. 'I'm Iron Eyes' betrothed. We're almost hitched. Me and him is nearly man and wife.'

'How'd you figure that?' McGee asked their captive.

'He wrestled with my chests,' she sniffed. 'Where I'm from that means something.'

McGee looked at Vance. Both men frowned.

'Let's get a better look at them chests of yours, Squirrel.' Denver marched up to Sally and ripped her already tattered shirt from her and laughed brutishly as she tried to conceal her modesty. A satisfied smirk traced his hardened features as he tossed the shirt at Vance who caught it and raised it to his face.

'She sure smells mighty sweet,' Vance sighed before tucking the trophy into his shirt. 'She smells just like a woman.'

'Ain't that a surprise?' Denver rolled

his eyes and moved back to the open door. He grabbed one of the rifles and cranked its mechanism. His narrowed eyes studied the clearing carefully and then noted that the sun had fallen below the trees. 'We gotta make sure that Iron Eyes sees her before he sees us. I want that stinking galoot to be so riled up at the sight of his woman strapped to a chair that he charges into the clearing without thinking.'

Both Vance and McGee laughed.

'Then we kill him?' McGee grinned.

'Yep, then we can kill the bastard in our crossfire. There ain't no cover between here and the trees and that's exactly where I want him. Out in the open so we can blast him into a million bits.' Denver sighed heavily as his fingers grabbed bullets from an open cardboard box and began sliding them into the rifle's magazine.

'Iron Eyes don't die that easy, old timer,' Sally glared at Denver. 'He'll kill you all before you can get him in your gunsights.'

Jody Denver took a backward step and then unleashed his free hand at the defiant Sally.

'Hush up or I'll gag you,' Denver slapped the restrained female. Her beautiful head rocked on her slender neck as her golden hair bounced from the impact. Sally raised her head and stared defiantly at the outlaw leader as blood trickled from the corner of her mouth.

McGee picked up a rifle and stepped closer to Denver.

'She might be right. Iron Eyes ain't no fool, Jody. Just how are we gonna make sure that he leaves them trees?' he asked.

'He'll come out of them trees, Bill,' Denver said as he watched the light begin to fade out in the clearing. 'I reckon that when he spots his woman buck-naked and looking the worse for wear, he'll be so riled that he won't give his own hide a second thought. It'll be a turkey shoot.'

Vance dried his mouth on the back of

his sleeve and then paced to the side of both his comrades. He lifted the last of the rifles off the table and stared over the shoulders of his fellow outlaws out into the clearing.

'You mean you want me and Bill to stay out there in the trees all night waiting for a galoot who might not even turn up?' he sighed shaking his head. 'I ain't no coward but I don't cotton to staying out there all night with wild critters looking for their next meal.'

McGee looked terrified, 'There's bin a mountain lion roaming around here the last couple of nights, Jody.'

'That's right,' Vance nodded. 'I took a couple of pot-shots at it the night before last. That critter is probably even more dangerous than Iron Eyes.'

'Nothing is more dangerous than Iron Eyes,' Squirrel Sally smirked at them. 'You'll find that out the hard way. When he shows up you'll be wishing it was a mountain lion.'

The look which Denver bestowed upon his men was enough to end any further objections or conversation. He pointed to the left and then the right.

'Take up positions,' Denver drawled.

Vance moved through the twilight and secreted himself in the trees at the edge of the clearing while McGee raced to the large woodpile ten yards from their secured horses. The outlaw lay on the ground behind the carefully chopped and stacked logs.

Denver turned and looked at Sally.

She did not like the smile on his unshaven face. It did not suit his scowling features and troubled the female. She raised her knees in a vain bid to hide from his prying eyes as he slowly moved toward her.

'Keep your damn distance,' Sally said in a vain bid to stop the veteran outlaw. 'I'm betrothed to Iron Eyes and he's not the sort of critter who looks kindly on folks getting close to his woman.'

Her valiant bluff fell on deaf ears. He grabbed her arms and hauled her off the cabin floor and then pushed her on to the only chair in the room. He removed his bandanna from his neck and tied one of her ankles to a chair leg. Denver stepped to the table as she rocked on the chair.

'That should hold you.' He chuckled.

Sally glared at him through her golden hair.

'It's getting dark fast,' Denver lifted the glass funnel off the oil lamp and scratched a match across the surface of the rough table and cupped its flame. 'I want your man to get a good look at his woman.'

She watched as Denver lit the lamp's wick, then returned the funnel and adjusted its brass wheel. The cabin lit up like the fourth of July as lamplight cascaded around the confines of the small cabin.

The flickering light danced upon her exposed flesh. Sally lowered her head as she tried to work out how to get the better of the three men when she was hog-tied.

The hardened outlaw had placed her directly opposite the open doorway. With the amber light dancing on her seated form it suddenly became obvious to Sally that Denver intended Iron Eyes to see her clearly as he reached the edge of the trees and rush to her aide.

Denver sat upon one of the crude cots and rested his back against the log wall with his Winchester resting upon his knees as he stared out of the window.

Although Sally was bathed in the unforgiving light of the oil lamp she was determined to free herself from her bonds before Iron Eyes fell into Denver's trap.

Having her shirt torn from her flesh had loosened the leather belts grip and it had moved upward slightly. She wriggled and felt the leather continue to ride up her arms' naked flesh steadily. Sally only paused when Denver glanced in her direction. Another few inches and she could free herself from the belt and make a dash for her Winchester, she reasoned.

When Denver's gaze returned to the window she continued to gently manipulate the belt with her arms and shoulders as the toes of her free foot picked at the bandanna's knot. Sally knew that her prized rifle was just outside the door waiting for her to unleash its fury.

So near and yet so far away.

As Sally continued to discreetly manipulate the belt, she began to realize that the four paces to the open doorway were probably four paces too far but she was willing to risk her life for the man she adored. Her beautiful eyes glanced through her long wavy hair at Denver.

His finger was curled around the trigger of his rifle ready to start shooting. He'd kill her for sure. Sally knew that she was the only target in the cabin until her beloved Iron Eyes arrived.

The belt's progress suddenly halted. She looked down and then frowned at her perfectly formed breasts. They were preventing the leather restraint from continuing its upward journey.

Undeterred she inhaled and discreetly pressed on.

14

With arrows still flying at his wide back, Iron Eyes rammed his bloody spurs into the valiant stallion and gave out a yell that was even louder than those of the Kiowa riders behind him. The powerful golden stallion had continued to prove its pedigree and breeding against the Indian ponies who could not keep pace with its superior strength. With its gaunt rider balanced precariously in its stirrups, the mighty animal raced to the foot of the precarious slope.

The palomino began to ascend its muddy surface at incredible pace. Iron Eyes kept whipping the tail of the stallion and shouting at the muscular steed. The intrepid horse responded to the encouragement and kept on climbing.

Its shod hoofs clawed at the mud and continued to climb up the almost vertical obstacle with the dexterity more akin to a mountain goat. The stallion's muscles rippled as it kept moving up through the slippery mud in response to the gaunt horseman's vocal and physical encouragement.

Within a mere heartbeat, the horse was halfway up the slope. Its horseshoes dug into the soft mud and found every scrap of resistance to use as a ladder. The large palomino used the tree roots which lay just inches beneath the mud as rungs of the natural ladder and ascended them speedily as its master balanced by gripping the silver horn of the Mexican saddle.

Like an accomplished tightrope walker, Iron Eyes shook spent casings from one of his guns and then plunged the smoking weapon back into his bullet-filled dust coat pocket.

With the dexterity of a well-seasoned riverboat cardsharp, the bounty hunter managed to fill its chambers with fresh bullets from the depths of his pocket. As the lean bounty hunter remained standing above the shoulders of his intrepid horse, his bony digits secured the rotating chamber back into the belly of the Navy Colt.

Iron Eyes glanced over his shoulder at the Kiowa as they swarmed between the trees before reaching the foot of the slope. He licked his dry lips and watched as some of the braves plucked arrows from the mud and trees to replenish their quivers.

He lashed the tail of the horse.

'Keep moving, horse,' he yelled as he sat back down and spurred the exhausted animal. 'You're almost there. C'mon, you can do it.'

His heart was pounding inside his battle-scarred chest like a war drum as he stared at the top of the slope slowly getting closer. The dishevelled horseman did everything he could think of to encourage the palomino up the last few precarious yards. Then he heard the Kiowa start their bone-chilling chant once again.

Iron Eyes glanced back at the Indians. They had remounted and were attempting to follow the larger horse up the slippery rise. But unlike their prey, the Kiowa were riding bareback and needed both hands to prevent themselves from sliding backwards off their ponies.

The freshly reloaded Navy Colt fired down at the Kiowa. His shot found the lead rider and punched him off the back of his painted pony. Both horse and rider fell back and took other horsemen with them.

Iron Eyes turned carefully and pounded the gun against his canteens. The stallion reacted and hastened its speed.

There was no time to lose, the skeletal Iron Eyes told himself as he pushed the smoking six-gun into his belt. He had to reach the top of the slope before his pursuers started to use his wide back for target practice once more.

With one hand gripping the silver saddle horn the other gathered the ends of his long leathers and started to whip the palomino's shoulders mercilessly.

'Keep going, you ornery gluepot,' he ranted. 'You nearly done it, boy.'

The beleaguered stallion drove its

hoofs into the muddy slope and gave its last valiant effort. Every sinew of the animal rippled in the fading light as it forced itself up and over the slippery ridge. With its legs covered in mud up to its knees, the palomino had managed to clear the lip of the slope. Level ground greeted the palomino as it fell forward on to its knees.

The exhausted horse just lay on the ground for a few moments on the grassy ground as its snorted. Then it summoned every last ounce of its strength and got back to its feet. For a few seemingly endless moments the stallion swayed like a newly-born foal.

Iron Eyes patted the neck of the weary horse, looped his leg over its neck and slid to the ground. He could hear the mayhem of the chasing Indians below his high vantage point as he pulled out his other gun and swiftly reloaded it with more of the loose bullets from his pockets.

'Them Injuns sure ain't happy, horse,' he growled as he strode to the very edge of the slope and stared down at the Kiowa braves. 'Get going. I'll kill you if you don't.'

The determined braves looked up at the haunting figure above them. They could not believe that the horseman had managed to climb the greasy slope while they had failed. The legend of the mysterious Iron Eyes only grew in their collective minds.

Was he truly a living corpse? Was that why they had failed to kill him? How had his horse done what their own ponies could not?

Iron Eyes' icy stare watched as the frantic Kiowa unsuccessfully attempted to navigate the same route as he had taken. Half had fallen from their ponies while the remainder were bogged down in the mire.

As his bony hands toyed with the Navy Colt he observed a few of the fallen warriors at the foot of the hill raising their bows and firing at him. It sounded like crazed hornets as the arrows flew from their bowstrings.

Like a ragged scarecrow Iron Eyes stepped back as arrows flew past him and hit overhanging branches. As leaves rained down on the bounty hunter, he drew his second six-shooter.

He cocked the hammers of both weapons until they fully locked into position and then advanced back to the edge of the rim. The tall haunting figure had only just stopped when he heard the sound of a bow releasing another arrow.

Before he could retreat the arrow came up from the blackness below him. Its flint arrowhead came within inches of his face and hit the rim of the wide sombrero he had been wearing since leaving Mexico.

The wide brimmed hat was torn from his head. Its drawstring snapped under his chin. Iron Eyes watched as the sombrero went hurtling off into the impenetrable depths of the forest. Startled and angry the lean bounty hunter gritted his teeth and moved back to the very edge of the slope.

'Damn it all,' Iron Eyes growled as he

glared down at the highly painted warriors who were gathering up their bows and placing arrows on the taut strings. 'That arrow almost hit me.'

His words only drew more venomous arrows.

With his primed guns still gripped in his bony hands, Iron Eyes ducked as half a dozen more lethal projectiles flew up from the floor of the gully and passed all around his emaciated body. A fury raged up inside the crouching bounty hunter like an erupting volcano.

The bounty hunter fired his weapons in quick succession down into the depths of the gully at his determined adversaries.

Yet the gloom hindered his usual expert marksmanship. His narrowed eyes had seen at least three of the Kiowa fall before the acrid gunsmoke spewing from his gun barrels made it impossible to see his attackers any longer. Yet Iron Eyes kept on firing into the acrid smoke.

After emptying both guns, Iron Eyes stepped back from the edge of the slope, shook the spent casings from his smoking weapons and silently reloaded each Navy Colt in turn.

Then he heard the ponies riding away and pocketed both guns into his dust coat pocket. The Kiowa had gathered their dead and wounded and then retreated before the guns of the bounty hunter began spitting more death at them.

Like a demonic creature from the bowels of Hell, he turned and paced back to the side of his exhausted mount. He had no desire to look down into the abyss and see the bloody carnage he had just created. Iron Eyes had seen death too many times to be curious about it.

He patted the palomino on the neck, grabbed the reins before stepping back into his stirrup and hauling his pitifully thin body back up on to the ornate saddle. His thoughts returned to the reason he was in this unholy forest at all.

It was imperative that he find Squirrel Sally before she encountered equally dangerous foes. The bounty hunter was dog-tired but there was no time to rest. He glanced up at the sky and shook his head. The blue heavens were getting darker with every passing second and he was not sure whether that was good or bad for his quest.

Iron Eyes turned the stallion and stared at the giant trees that faced him. There was no hint of remorse in his emotionless face for what had just occurred. Iron Eyes had been attacked and had fought his attackers.

It was as simple as that.

There was nothing personal in it.

His only regret was that he had wasted valuable ammunition for no good reason apart from defending himself. Ammunition that might be required to kill wanted outlaws who had a price on their heads. He tapped the flanks of his mount and allowed the exhausted stallion to walk forward.

There was no profit in killing anyone apart from outlaws he thought as he glanced over his shoulder and shouted out at the fleeing Kiowa.

'That'll teach you to mess with a man

fresh out of hard liquor,' he shouted over his shoulder. 'I don't mind you shooting my hat but not when my damn head's in it.'

The horse continued to slowly make its way through the thick grass between the trees when Iron Eyes suddenly spotted something ahead.

It was something that he had not seen in quite a while.

The bounty hunter tapped his boots harder against the flanks of his mount. The horse trotted through the maze of trees until it reached the spot that its master had noticed in the fading light.

Iron Eyes stared down at the trail road and then rubbed his sweat-soaked brow. He could no longer remember the last time he had seen the road. Glimpses of moonlight filtered through the tree branches and sparkled on the road as frost began to coat its surface.

His eyes tightened and focused on the wheel grooves on the frosty road. He nodded in satisfaction and then stared down at the familiar grooves glinting in the sparkling moonlight.

'That's Squirrel Sally's stagecoach tracks, horse,' he growled and steadied the palomino as his eyes strained and studied the trail road as it led up the hillside deeper into the forest. 'I'm closing in on that little chilli-pepper. When I find her I'll be able to get my hands on my golden eagles and drink all her whiskey before kicking her butt.'

With renewed resolve, Iron Eyes encouraged the palomino to start trotting and looked around the dense undergrowth which surrounded him. As the exhausted stallion continued up the trail and rounded a bend, the bounty hunter caught the scent of smoke in his flared nostrils. Mist made it impossible to see the smoke that his nose had already identified. He eased back on his reins and stopped the stallion.

Iron Eyes sniffed the cooling evening air and held the horse in check for a few moments as his keen senses tried to work out where the smoke was coming from.

He frowned.

'That's coming from a smoke stack,' he said. 'That means there's a cabin up here someplace.'

The bounty hunter instinctively knew that the smell of smoke was coming off the mountain from a place he had yet to reach or discover. Iron Eyes gathered up his reins as he thought of Squirrel Sally again.

No matter how hard the emaciated bounty hunter tried, he could not rid his mind of the tempestuous female. He kept telling himself that he was simply chasing his small fortune in golden coins but in truth Squirrel was far more precious to the brutalized bounty hunter.

Suddenly he heard the howls of a distant timber wolf.

It echoed all around him and sent a cold shiver up his spine as he looked all around him. Iron Eyes had not even considered that there might be wild animals in this vast forest until he had heard the wolf baying at the large moon.

'Damn it all,' he cursed as he steadied

the horse. 'First there was back-shooters, then Injuns and now wild critters. What next?'

Iron Eyes cracked his long leathers and carried on up the trail road through the eerie light of the rising moon. His bony hands replaced his spent bullets with fresh ones and then poked the six-shooters back into his belt.

The stallion had only travelled a few miles through the moonlight when something else caught his attention on the trail road. Iron Eyes slowed the muscular mount and narrowed his eyes as the horse slowly trotted to what he was looking at.

His scrawny hands pulled back on the long leathers and slowed the stallion. As the palomino reached the abandoned stagecoach, Iron Eyes drew back on his reins and looped them around the saddle horn.

Iron Eyes felt his heart pounding inside his chest as the high-shouldered animal came to a halt. Sally should be with her prized stagecoach but she was nowhere to be seen, he thought. Where was she?

He dismounted silently as every fibre of his being knew his feisty friend would not desert her precious stage-coach willingly. Iron Eyes moved like a nervous panther and approached the coach. He rested his hand upon its tailgate and glanced at the ground.

His eyes focused on the ground as frost sparkled upon the marks left by the last people to move across its surface. He knelt and studied the boot prints.

'Three men,' Iron Eyes muttered before looking at the impressions closer to the back of the coach. He gritted his teeth and leaned down until his face was only ten inches above the ground. 'Sally was kneeling and then dragged off.'

He did not want to believe the tracks he had just read.

Iron Eyes returned to his full height. He shook his head and then walked along the vehicle before stopping beside the carriage door. He looked into the coach but Squirrel Sally was not there. He had hoped to see her sleeping, but knew she had been taken by someone.

All the bounty hunter knew for sure was that whoever had taken his precious Squirrel were not Indians. The boots gave that away.

He raised his hand and ran his bony fingers through his hair and forced it off his face. A sudden thought filled him with dread.

What if they had killed her?

A fury suddenly rose up inside the gaunt bounty hunter as he strode across the frosty ground following the tracks into the undergrowth. He stopped at the edge of the treeline and stared into the blackness as his pulse rate increased.

He snapped his fingers.

The golden stallion walked wearily toward him and stopped at his shoulder. The large horse nudged the bounty hunter and snorted.

'Somebody took Squirrel, horse,' he rasped angrily. 'They might have killed her for all I know. If they have, I'll surely kill them.'

Iron Eyes turned and ran to the front of the stagecoach and climbed up to the driver's seat. He swung his legs over and rested his hip on the long sprung board. The bright moon filled the box with its eerie illumination. His fiery eyes stared down into the box to where Sally kept her most precious things. Within seconds he found the small leather bag, loosened its leather lace and stared at the golden eagles.

Yet even holding the weighty bag meant nothing to Iron Eyes. All he could think about was the short flame-headed beauty he had christened 'Squirrel'. He dropped the bag of coins back into the box and then found her whiskey bottle.

He loosened its cork and downed a quarter of its contents quickly in a vain attempt to calm himself down. Yet no amount of the amber liquor was enough to achieve that goal. He pushed the cork back into the clear neck of the bottle and dropped it into one of his pockets.

He was about to return to his horse

when he saw something at the end of the long driver's seat. It was her pipe.

His bony digits touched it. It was ice cold.

Iron Eyes exhaled loudly and felt his outrage growing. He had tried to remain calm, but something inside his tortured soul refused to remain detached from the situation.

'Squirrel,' he repeated her name several times and then raised his head. No creature this side of Hell could have been more dangerous than Iron Eyes was as he climbed down from the high vantage point.

He had a fire burning inside him. A fire that was out of control. His narrowed eyes were red as he marched back to his awaiting horse and picked up its long leathers.

The bounty hunter reached up, grabbed his saddle horn and then mounted the palomino. He drove both boots into his stirrups and then tapped his boots against the flanks of the stallion.

'C'mon, horse,' he hissed like a

serpent about to strike out at its unsuspecting victim. 'Let's go find that little gal.'

As the high-shouldered stallion walked into the trees, the stern-faced bounty hunter pulled a cigar from his pocket and pushed it into the corner of his scarred lips. His thumbnail scratched the tip of a match and raised its flame to the end of the cigar. He filled his lungs with the acrid smoke and then allowed it to slowly escape through his teeth. As it trailed out into the cold air he tossed the match at the frost-covered ground and then pulled the whiskey bottle from his deep trail coat pocket.

He leaned back and lifted a satchel flap and then dropped the bottle into its empty void. The gruesome bounty hunter did not need any more whiskey to fuel his volcanic temper as countless emotions raged through his veins. Iron Eyes was like a stick of dynamite as its fuse burned toward its detonator cap. His half closed eyes darted all around him in search of the three men who had taken his precious Squirrel Sally.

The Denver gang had made a mistake.

They had taken Sally in order to lure her man into their crossfire. Like so many others before them, they had underestimated the sheer fury of the notorious Iron Eyes. They had considered him to be like all the others of his blood-thirsty profession.

That was a mistake.

Iron Eyes was different. He had always ridden with death as his constant companion. For some unknown reason, death had always protected him in his pursuit of the wanted men the law was incapable of finding. A dark omen shielded the gaunt horseman as he allowed the tall palomino to navigate through the forest in search of his prey.

What troubled Iron Eyes was that its protection might not be shared by the petite Sally Cooke. Squirrel Sally might have already fallen foul of the Grim Reaper's retribution. The thought chilled the wounded bounty hunter.

'They'd better not have hurt Squirrel,' he muttered as the palomino made its way deeper into the trees. With every step the bounty hunter sucked in smoke and stared at the boot prints he was following. 'You ain't gonna escape, amigos. I'm the best tracker there ever was. You got my Squirrel and I'm gonna kill you.'

Iron Eyes allowed the weary horse to find its own pace as it made its way between the trees. As the horse quietly strode on through the forest, its master listened out for any clues to how close he was to his prey.

His long fingers pulled the spent cigar from his mouth and tossed it aside. He rubbed his face and then saw a trail of chimney smoke rising from the trees and curling up into the moonlight. He was getting closer, he thought.

Soon he would get them in his gunsights and teach them a permanent lesson. If they had harmed one hair on Squirrel's head, he would make their journey to Hell a slow, lingering ordeal.

Iron Eyes could not see the cabin through the barrier of trees and undergrowth but he could smell it. He was like a ravenous wild animal with the scent of his chosen targets in his nostrils. He tapped his boots against the flanks of the exhausted stallion and urged it on.

They would pay for their actions, he vowed.

Iron Eyes allowed the tall palomino to continue heading toward the smell of wood smoke. As thorny brambles tore at his already mutilated flesh, the unblinking horseman continued on oblivious to everything except finding his beautiful female companion and confronting her captors.

Then his narrowed eyes caught sight of the lamplight as it cascaded from the cabin and wove a path through the trees toward him. A haunting smile etched his horrific features as he slowly drew closer to the clearing. Every sinew in his wounded body wanted to ride at them with his guns blazing and show them no mercy, but Squirrel Sally was there. He lowered his head and glared through his long limp hair at the trees and the cabin. The powerful stallion walked on toward the clearing as if it knew exactly where its master intended for it to go.

The claw-like hands of the beleaguered bounty hunter checked his guns.

'They're gonna pay big time,' Iron Eyes hissed.

15

The forest which surrounded the remote cabin suddenly fell silent as if the wild animals that lived within its confines recognized the smell of death as it moved silently through the trees. The moonlit heavens were suddenly filled with birds as they fled the approach of the ominous Iron Eyes. Yet the bounty hunter kept on coming toward the lamplight like a moth drawn to a naked flame.

Within the logger's shelter, Jody Denver warmed his bones against the stove in blissful ignorance that the scourge of all men of his dubious occupation was getting nearer with every beat of his ruthless heart.

It had been hours since the three outlaws had set their trap and waited for the legendary Iron Eyes to stumble into their crossfire. The night had brought a bone-biting chill which gnawed at their bones. McGee and Vance had drawn the short straws and were huddled out in the cold courtyard that surrounded the small cabin, while their brutish leader sat on a cot close to the wood burning stove. Yet with both the window and door wide open, the cabin was little warmer than it was outside.

The long wait was wearing all three outlaws down as much as the dropping temperature. They all began to doubt that the notorious bounty hunter was going to show at all. Minutes had turned into hours and the forest grew ever colder as the last three surviving members of the Denver gang waited.

The cabin was bathed in the flickering amber light of the lamp set upon the small table close to the open doorway. Sally remained seated on the hardback chair directly before the door.

'Where the hell is he?' Denver growled as he flexed his fingers. 'I thought you said that Iron Eyes was following you, Squirrel.'

'He is,' Sally said without moving a muscle.

'I'm starting to think that you're just a little gal with a real big mouth,' Denver got to his feet and moved to the stove as he glanced over his shoulder at her. 'I'll bet you don't even know Iron Eyes at all. This has all bin a pack of lies to stop me and the boys from having our way with you.'

The golden haired female gave a slight laugh. 'Like I told you, I'm the betrothed of Iron Eyes. He's coming and when he finds out what you done to me, he'll be mighty angry.'

'Bull,' Denver shouted across the cabin. 'You're just a real smart little gal. I'm beginning to think that we should forget all about waiting for your betrothed and do what we want with you.'

Sally did not say anything.

'I'm gonna call the boys back in here,' Denver opened the black stove door and pushed two logs onto its crimson heart. 'I reckon that they've earned the right to pleasure you after spending the last couple of hours freezing their long-johns off out there.'

Sally stared at the open door. She began to wonder if Denver was right about Iron Eyes not trailing her. Her doubts did not last long though as her keen hunter's eyesight caught a glimpse of something moving in the trees. Although she could not make out the approaching rider perfectly, she knew that it could only be Iron Eyes.

'You should call them back in here,' Sally bluffed Denver without turning her head to look at him. 'I ain't feared of any of you.'

Denver moved with his rifle cradled between his hands to where Sally sat. He grabbed her mane of hair, jerked her head back and looked down at her beautiful face.

'What game are you playing, missy?' he riled. 'Nobody can be as calm as you are. Are you so dumb that you can't see how dangerous me and the boys are?'

There was no expression on Sally's

face. She just looked into Denver's troubled features blankly. He released his grip.

Sally watched the elder outlaw pace to the open doorway and stare out into the clearing and the trees that fringed it. Unlike herself, Denver did not notice the approach of the mysterious horseman.

He paced back to the stove and opened its iron door again. The heat felt good to the outlaw as he warmed his hands before the crackling flames. Denver turned his head and saw the emotionless face of Sally staring at him from the chair.

'What you looking at?' Denver snapped at her.

Sally sighed, 'I'm looking at a critter who'll more than likely be dead before sun-up.'

Denver forced a smile and then picked up his Winchester again and pointed its long metal barrel at the unconcerned female. The rifle shook with every word he uttered.

'Shut the hell up, Squirrel,' he

stammered. 'I could have killed you back at your stagecoach but figured me and the boys might get some pleasure out of you. But I warn you, it don't matter to me if'n you're dead or alive.'

Sally shook her long wavy hair back and smiled at the rafters. She then raised an eyebrow and stared straight at the outlaw fearlessly.

'Kill me then,' she taunted. 'It don't matter none to me.'

Jody Denver marched from the stove and stood over her half naked body. He pushed the barrel into the side of her neck and panted like an old hound dog. He was angry enough to kill her but women were scarce in these parts and no matter how annoying Sally was, he could not allow himself to waste anything quite so precious.

'I should pull the trigger,' he threatened. 'But that would be too easy. I'm gonna make you beg to be killed, girl. When me and the boys are through with you, you'll be begging for us to end your misery.'

Defiantly, Sally tilted her head and smiled.

'You and them half-wits out in the yard ain't gonna be doing nothing except dying, old timer,' Sally said calmly before turning her head and then fluttering her eyelashes at the anxious Denver. 'Iron Eyes will kill you when he gets here. If you harm me, he'll kill you real slow.'

Her words burrowed into the hardened outlaw. Somehow she refused to be intimidated and that not only confused Denver, it also troubled him. Squirrel Sally was unlike any female he had ever encountered. He began to realize that she was probably telling the truth about being Iron Eyes' woman. She seemed totally unafraid as he imagined any female belonging to the infamous bounty hunter would be.

Denver backed away from Sally and lowered his rifle. His face was twitching as his mind raced. He rubbed his sweating face along the back of his sleeve and tried to figure out why the tiny female was so confident.

'You're plumb loco, Squirrel,' he spat as he clutched his rifle and stared at his captive. 'I ain't never met a gal as loco as you. You're crazy enough to belong to Iron Eyes.'

Sally sniffed the evening air and then started to nod.

'Maybe I am loco,' she agreed. 'But my nose tells me that my betrothed is headed this way.'

Denver's rugged face suddenly went pale. He moved back toward her and circled the chair until he was directly before her. He bent forward.

'You can smell him?' he asked fearfully.

She nodded. 'Yep, I can smell him OK.'

Denver moved closer to her.

'Are you serious?'

'I sure am,' Sally answered. 'Iron Eyes carries the smell of death with him. Can't you smell it?'

Denver swung around on his heels and moved to the open doorway. He gripped his rifle firmly as he looked out into the clearing. He inhaled the cool air through his flared nostrils but could not smell the acrid stench which he expected to detect.

The outlaw had his back to Sally as his eyes nervously scanned the surrounding trees for any sign of the lethal Iron Eyes. The petite female pushed the bandanna off her ankle and quietly stood up.

It took only one last wiggle of her shapely torso to free herself of the leather restraint. As the belt reached her shoulders she raised her hands and silently unbuckled it. She allowed the long strap to fall at her side and then gripped it firmly.

'Hey, old timer,' Sally whispered in her most alluring tone. 'I'm ready now.'

Denver turned. The metal buckle struck him across his face as the fiery female swung it with all her might. The impact sent the outlaw staggering sideways. He collided with the door and then crashed on to the floor.

Blood splattered across the floorboards as the dazed Denver tried to gather his wits. Sally jumped forward and kicked the outlaw as hard as her bare foot would allow and then leapt over the table and dived through the open window.

Sally landed on the dirt, quickly raced to her trusty Winchester which was still resting against the cabin front wall and snatched it. She pushed the hand guard down and then saw the shivering McGee looking at her from behind the pile of stacked logs.

For a split second they both stared at one another in bewilderment. Then Sally fired the repeating rifle at the young outlaw. The bullet hit the freshly stacked logs and showered sawdust over the startled McGee.

The outlaw ducked as his cold hands fumbled for his own rifle. Before McGee was able to lift his Winchester and look over the logs, Sally had darted for cover.

'What was that?' Vance yelled out as he came running to his cohort. 'What the hell were you shooting at, Bill?'

'The girl,' McGee exclaimed as his eyes searched for her. 'She did the shooting. She come out of that window like a jack rabbit, grabbed her rifle and fired at me.'

Vance cocked his own rifle and looked beyond their skittish horses to where he had caught a glimpse of the half-naked female running. He squinted and grabbed the collar of his fellow outlaw.

'Let's check Denver,' he said. 'The way she's running I got a feeling that she might've killed him.'

McGee trailed Vance back to the open doorway. The flickering light of the lamp revealed the stunned Denver on the ground. Droplets of blood covered the door and floor from the injuries Sally had inflicted upon the groggy outlaw leader.

McGee looked down upon Denver as he held his face and looked up at his two men. 'What happened, Jody?'

'Damned if I know,' Denver admitted as they helped him clamber back to his feet. He held his bleeding face and blinked a few times. 'Where'd she go?'

Vance pointed. 'She ran into the forest.'

'You've got a mean cut there, Jody,'

McGee said as he looked at the bleeding gash across Denver's face. 'She must have hit you with the belt.'

Denver sighed and rested a hand on the table. 'I'm starting to think she was telling the truth about being Iron Eyes' woman, boys. No normal female would have the grit to even try doing that.'

'She almost blew my head off,' McGee stammered.

'She sure is a peppy little critter,' Vance added as Denver straightened up and wiped the blood from his face. 'A man could get himself killed getting frisky to something like that.'

'I'm gonna kill that bitch,' Denver growled as he grabbed his Winchester and pressed the palm of his hand against the savage gash. 'Nobody does this to me and lives to brag about it. That buckle nearly blinded me.'

The still dazed Denver moved back to the door when a bullet cut across the clearing and hit the wall. All three men ducked as clumps of wood flew in all directions.

'That little vixen is shooting at us,' Vance shouted as another bullet hit the door frame.

Denver blew out the oil lamp and carefully looked to where the shots had come from. 'That gal is a real pain in the backside, boys. She ain't gonna be satisfied until she kills us.'

McGee walked to the open window and peered out. 'She's got herself pretty good cover. From out there she got the door and the window covered. If we even try to leave the cabin she'll pick us off.'

Denver shook his head angrily.

'No she won't,' he snarled. 'No little runt is ever gonna pin Jody Denver down, boys.'

'How do you intend stopping her, Jody?' Vance asked as he brushed splinters off his coat and watched the older outlaw pace around the confines of the cabin. 'Squirrel's got us trapped and she knows it. If any of us move too close to the window or the door she'll kill us.'

Denver rested a hip on the table edge

and brooded for a few moments as he tried to regain his thoughts. 'There's always a way, Dan. We just ain't figured it yet.'

'That rifle of hers is fully loaded,' McGee muttered. 'She can keep us pinned down for as long as she wants.'

'Or until Iron Eyes shows up,' Vance said drily.

Denver glanced at Vance. 'I'd forgotten about him. Damn, I don't cotton to being trapped in here if that bastard shows his ugly face.'

The sound of dry brush cracking across the clearing drew all three men's attention. They turned and stared out at the trees that fringed the clearing and saw movement in the dense brush. Denver moved away from the table and stood with his rifle gripped in his shaking hands. His heart raced as he caught sight of the eerie figure moving through the moonlight toward the cabin.

'Hell,' he squirmed as he patted both his cohorts and pointed at the unholy image which was moving slowly astride his huge horse toward them. 'He's here.'

McGee and Vance gripped their rifles.

'Iron Eyes!'

Finale

The eerie moonlight caught the branches of the trees as they parted to reveal the strangest sight any of the Denver gang had ever seen. The palomino stallion emerged from the undergrowth carrying its unmoving cargo toward the small cabin across the expanse of cleared ground.

Vance gripped the rifle in his trembling hands as he stared through the moonlight at the horseman.

'He ain't got a head,' the terrified outlaw yelled.

McGee started to shake as he too saw the unholy vision.

'He's right, Jody,' he shouted in near hysteria. 'Iron Eyes ain't got no head. Look at him. Look at the bastard.'

Denver screwed up his eyes. His vision was at least fifteen years older than his gang members and nowhere as clear. Then he also saw the unbelievable sight.

From inside the cabin door, it certainly appeared to the onlookers that the stallion was indeed carrying a headless horseman upon its high shoulders.

The limp dust coat was perched upon the saddle with its empty sleeves moving in the evening breeze. Denver cranked his rifle's hand guard and then swiftly raised the Winchester to his shoulder.

'Whatever that is, I'm killing it.' Denver spat.

He fired and sent a bullet straight through the chest of the long coat. Denver looked perplexed as he cocked and fired his rifle again.

Within seconds all three of the gang were emptying their Winchesters at the strange vision. The palomino stallion halted its advance as the coat fell from where it had been perched upon the ornate Mexican saddle.

Denver and his cohorts lowered their smoking rifles and stared in confusion at the coat as it floated slowly through the moonlight to the ground.

'You're gonna have to buy me a new coat,' Iron Eyes drawled as he stepped out of the shadows beside the cabin and aimed both his Navy Colts at them. 'Now drop them rifles.'

The three outlaws watched as the hideous bounty hunter moved closer to the cabin with his guns trained on their innards. They did as he said and dropped their smoking rifles at their feet.

'Now where's Squirrel?' Iron Eyes hissed like a rattler about to strike out at them. 'Where's my Squirrel?'

Denver and his men still had their gun belts strapped around their middles as they stepped out of the cabin into the moonlight.

'She's over there someplace,' Denver indicated with a tilt of his head. 'That woman of yours has bin taking pot shots at us for the last ten minutes.'

Iron Eyes lowered his head but continued to stare at them through his limp hair. 'She's still alive?'

'She's still alive,' Denver and his men moved apart. They kept their hands hovering above their holstered six-guns as Iron Eyes remained perfectly still. 'Now let us get to our horses and ride out of here or we'll draw down on you.'

Iron Eyes could see Squirrel Sally moving away from the trees with her prized Winchester still clutched in her hands as he lowered his guns. His eyes darted back to the trio of outlaws.

'I reckon that sounds fair,' he whispered.

Sally waved her rifle and drew his attention.

'They're the Denver gang, Iron Eyes,' Sally screamed across the clearing. 'They're wanted dead or alive.'

A slight smile came to the bounty hunter's tortured features as he noticed the panic on the three faces before him.

'I already knew that, Squirrel.'

Denver went for his six-gun first, quickly followed by Vance and McGee. As their guns cleared their holsters Iron Eyes raised his Navy Colts and started firing. All three of the outlaws twisted on their heels as his deadly accurate bullets ripped through them. As they hit the ground the young female reached his side and wrapped her arms around his waist.

'I knew you'd come to save me, Iron Eyes,' she gushed as tears of relief rolled down her cheeks.

'I didn't come looking for you, Squirrel,' Iron Eyes said as he stared down through the gunsmoke at the three dead outlaws a few feet away from him. 'I come looking for my golden eagles.'

She looked up into his stony face and smiled. 'You liar, I know that you trailed me all the way from Mexico up into the goddamn wilderness. Only someone in love would do that.'

Iron Eyes raised an eyebrow and looked down into her beautiful face. He sighed and then moved to his horse and patted its neck as he retrieved his bullet-ridden coat from the ground. He shook it and then slid it on. She moved to his side and grabbed his arm as he poked his smoking guns back into his deep pockets.

'How'd you get this stinking coat to sit on your horse?' she asked the tall figure.

'A couple of branches helped, Squirrel,' he muttered as he stared at the dead outlaws. 'I made a frame, put the coat over it and sent the horse to the cabin. I cut around the clearing to get the drop on them.'

She looked confused.

'How'd you get this big horse to walk to the cabin?' she wondered.

'That was easy,' Iron Eyes looked at her. 'I just told him what to do and he done it. He's pretty smart for a Mexican horse, come to think about it.'

She made no effort to hide her womanly assets from his unconcerned eyes and danced before him in the moonlight. Her flesh sparkled in the crisp evening air. Iron Eyes did not appear to notice her lack of clothing though.

'Are you thirsty?' Sally asked coyly.

'I already found your whiskey bottle,' he said as he headed for the corpses and draped them over their horses in turn. 'I already drunk most of it.'

As he finished securing the bodies to the horses, he returned his attention to the still smiling female. He looked deep into her eyes and waited.

'I've got a case of sipping whiskey in my stagecoach, Iron Eyes,' she said as her eyelashes fluttered like butterflies, 'A whole twelve bottles of real whiskey.'

He led the three mounts toward her and then stared into her impish face. 'I didn't see any case of whiskey in your stagecoach, Squirrel.'

Sally grinned. 'It's hid under one of the seats.'

'A whole case, huh?' Iron Eyes lashed the three outlaws' horses' leathers to his cantle and then mounted the palomino. He held out his hand to the young female and helped her climb up behind him. Sally wrapped her arms around his waist as he turned the exhausted stallion and started to retrace his trail back to her stagecoach. 'At least you spent my money on something good, Squir-rel.'

She cleared her throat. Iron Eyes looked back at her as he steered the stallion back into the forest.

'Now what do you want, Squirrel?' he asked.

'Didn't you notice something different about me?' she pressed her naked breasts into his back and squeezed even harder. 'Something kinda nice?'

He thought about her question for a moment.

'You combed your hair?' he asked.

Sally frowned in frustration.

'No, I ain't combed my damn hair,' she groaned. 'I ain't got a shirt on. I'm buck-naked apart from my britches. My chests is uncovered. What does that make you think about, dearest?'

'Oh that, I just figured you were getting forgetful,' Iron Eyes said as he guided the palomino back toward the stagecoach. He then felt her hand slip down, enter his pants pocket and start searching. 'No point in looking in there.

I'm clean out of cigars, Squirrel.'

She pressed her mouth against his ear, 'I ain't looking for cigars, you ugly galoot.'